Also by Julia C. Hoffman

Darkness Endured
Enemy Within

A SIMPLE SONG

SONG

AN EDIE SWIFT NOVEL

JULIA C. HOFFMAN

Cover Design by Chrissy Long
Cover Photo by Adam Dorn
Formatting by Christine Keleny

ISBN-13: 978-0-9963974-4-5

To Bill,

who has traveled the road
with me

Thanks

Thanks to Corie McAliley for reading my drafts and giving me invaluable feedback. Estela Calvo-Gil for translating portions of this book. Anne Hoffman-González for her assistance. The Dane County Sheriff's Office for trying to correct my police procedural mistakes (a fool's errand). Lourdes Venard for her excellent editing. Chrissy Long for another wonderful cover.

These people have tried their darndest to correct my mistakes, but since my name is on the cover, responsibility for mistakes is all mine.

Chapter 1

†

There was a shooting.

A boy was dead.

Flies swarmed around the blood that gushed from the boy.

All the people who were pushing against the police tape trying to get a closer look at the body guessed the cause of death—a bullet or bullets. Probably the noise they heard last night.

But the police weren't releasing details for the usual reasons, the family hadn't been notified. The medical examiner still had the autopsy to perform to determine cause of death.

Both true, yet somehow everyone knew that a young man had been gunned down. Fueled by uncertainty, wild rumors swirled throughout the town: it was two boys fighting it out over a girl, a drive-by shooting for the hell of it, definitely gang warfare, everyone knew gang activity was picking up in the area, or a drug deal gone wrong. Maybe it was even kids playing a modern version of the old "I've got a bigger one than you" with guns snuck out of the house. Then the rumors doubled back to that it was a targeted shooting for a gang initiation rite. The neighborhood speculation juggled all the possibilities and narrowed it down to one—it was obvious, gang fight over drug territory. What else could it be? Madison was turning into a big city with big-city problems, and Dane County was growing along with it. The city's problems were spilling over its boundaries becoming the county's problems—like last night's shooting.

The cops had a few ideas of their own about the crime, but their speculations were not for public consumption. For all anyone knew at the moment, it might have been that the boy was shot because it was August and south-central Wisconsin was experiencing an unusual sustained heat wave, and the shooter was hot and miserable and had to take it out on someone.

A witness to last night's shooting stated that he saw someone run behind the convenience store, and then seconds later heard the clanging of metal on metal. The only metal object the deputies found near the convenience store that fit that description was the dumpster behind the store.

Somebody had to dive into the dumpster to

search for a gun, which might or might not be there and which might or might not have been used in the shooting. That somebody turned out to be Detective Edie Swift—it was her turn.

Dumpster diving was a necessary evil. She looked at that metal box, picturing all the stuff that had been brewing for days and nights in that cooker during the stretch of hot August days, and cringed. She put on the non-latex gloves, knee-high boot coverings, took hold of the dumpster's side, pushed herself up, took a look around, and again thought that if the shooting had occurred at the gas station a quarter mile down the road some Madison Police officer would have the pleasure of dumpster diving. Edie took a deep breath of fresh air and dropped into the cesspool. The reality was worse. After she got the impulse to gag under control, she went to work.

Edie was methodical in sifting through the garbage. She waded to the shallowest end of the pile to use it as her staging area. She threw everything to one side and began her careful search. There were countless plastic bags of dog shit that neighbors didn't want to carry home to deposit in their own garbage, melted ice cream cones, slushies which coated everything, half-eaten bananas and hotdogs, stuff that was so dissolved that she couldn't identify it, a few newspapers, and used condoms—she found lots of those.

The rising heat of the day mingled with the putrid layers of escaping air hit Edie's nose. She felt the puke rising. She pushed her way through the garbage to the side of metal box, leaned over its edge, and puked. When there wasn't anything else to vomit, she climbed out, careful to avoid her breakfast, which was spreading across the concrete. She wiped puke from her face and caught a whiff of herself—God she stank. Edie looked at her wristwatch; it was a worthless half-hour search except that the dumpster diving duty now passed to someone else—that knowledge brightened her day. She'd found nothing that could be connected to the shooting—maybe the security camera caught something, was anyone checking it?

Despite Edie's dumpster odor she helped canvass the neighborhood for anyone else who might have seen or heard something from the night before. The few people at home said they were sleeping or thought it was kids setting off firecrackers—they rolled over in bed and went back to sleep. She noticed that people backed away from her during her inquiries, but their dogs were real friendly.

After the photos and measurements of the crime scene were completed, the detailed sweep of the area finished, it was time to go. Dumpster odors still clung to Edie. She looked at her car; there were still a few years of payments left before it was all hers. And it needed protection from her, something to keep the odors from seeping into the seats. Stripping down to her bra and undies crossed her mind. She rejected that possibility—it was okay when she was a teen, probably not okay as a Dane County Sheriff's detective. She could afford a newspaper to spread across the seat.

Edie guesstimated that it would take three newspapers to keep the dumpster stench away from car seats. Reluctantly she bought them. It wasn't so long ago when she could have bought breakfast, lunch, and dinner with that amount of money. She dug through her pockets for the correct change, put it on the counter. Taking a visual sweep of the store before leaving, she saw the clerk take a Kleenex and sweep the money into the cash register. What? Her money wasn't any good?

The newspapers were skimpy—news must be in short supply, maybe the shooting would change that, she thought. But it was for a good cause— saving her car from her body odor. Edie glanced at the headlines as she walked to her car. No need to read it, she knew the important stuff: the August heat wave was continuing into a second week with no relief in sight. Maybe a long swim in one of Madison's lakes would cool her off and take away some of the odor. Unfortunately, all her clothes were back in Troutbeck, and her skinny-dipping days looked as if they were in the past. Anyway, it was daytime and most of her skinny-dipping had been done at night. She'd have to sweat out this August heat like everyone else—running from air-conditioned car to an air-conditioned building.

Edie leaned against her car paging through the newspaper; she didn't find any story of last night's shooting. It happened in the wee hours of the morning, she reasoned—probably too late to make the papers. Edie looked up as she turned the page and watched reporters on the other side of the police tape work for their stories. Leigh Stone was wrapping up her news flash; farther down the block Mark Uselman was taking notes as a resident gave local color for his story. But nearby residents reported that the gas station was well known for its drug dealings; on certain nights, the locals steered clear of the area. They were surprised no one had been shot sooner. Edie raised the paper to just below eye level; a quick glance down would prevent anyone from making contact with her.

Still, a little sympathy for Uselman and even for Stone crept into her thoughts; the reporters needed something to fill out the usual police blurb. The police weren't releasing details of last night's shooting—even though they were certain it wasn't a random shooting, they had no concern for the public's safety.

Edie got up the courage to spread the newspapers on the seat; she promised the car that it would get a deluxe cleaning inside and out. She got into her car; there was work to do. Last night's shooting brought the grand total to two in one week.

All that could be gotten from her morning's work was that another boy was dead and somewhere in Madison another mama joined the rising chorus of brokenhearted cries.

Chapter 2

†

A path opened for Edie as she walked through the downtown sheriff's station on her way to the locker room and showers. She placed her valuables in her locker, stripped off her clothes and double bagged them, then walked to the showers. Normally showering at the station was a quick in and out for her, but not today—the stench of the dumpster kept oozing out of her skin. She scrubbed and scrubbed, yet the smell lingered. Finally, she called it quits, turned off the water, and toweled off, but a faint dumpster odor persisted. She double bagged the towels before throwing them into the hazardous waste bin.

Her bag of clothes still sat in front of her locker; apparently no one wanted to touch it either. She kicked it off to the side and put on the spare set of clothes she kept in her locker for times like this.

No one greeted Edie when she walked into the staff room. Everyone's head was down, busy typing into the computer their own reports of the morning activities that detailed their part of the in-vestigation, who got interviewed, what they said, heard, and saw, where the person was at the time. The why of the crime hadn't officially been discovered. Once in a while a deputy would sit back, grab a pencil to chew on while they checked their report, delete some stuff, write again, and recheck it before sending it to the higher-ups to review.

Edie sat down to type her part of the morning. She paused for a moment as she decided how to write it. She could make it a comedy ending with her puking her guts out. Or a straightforward report of when she got in and out of the dumpster, tacking on a laundry list of her dumpster findings. Or one the DA, the facts-only department, would accept. She could feel the tension in the room rising; no one liked writing these reports—they had come for the action. She needed to get her report done and get out on the street before the room exploded in spitballs and rubber band fights. She decided on a straightforward report.

Only the facts were written, but Edie couldn't resist adding the dumpster incident or the spreading puke—the higher-ups needed to be reminded that cops were people and the job wasn't easy, especially these days. Respect for police officers had eroded since last year's shooting of a young unarmed black man. Everyone was still cautious—the public and the police.

Done with her report, Edie relaxed and glanced around the room. It looked as if everyone was having a bad case of writer's block—they were leaning back in their chairs, staring at their computers. In another era they'd be chewing on their pens and ripping their reports in half only to begin again.

"Someone give me some help, I need a good opening sentence," moaned a frustrated deputy.

"It was a dark..."

"No, it was a steamy morning..."

"How about it was hot enough to fry eggs?"

"It was the best of times..."

"For those of you who weren't in the dumpster," Edie added to the suggestions.

"Save it for your novels, you guys, the DA only wants the facts," shouted Steve, who was pounding away at his computer.

"Edie, was that a new scent you are trying out this morning?" someone shouted, anything to keep from writing.

"Thought there was the unmistakable scent of eau de garbage in the room," yelled Steve from across the room.

Comments on Edie's dumpster odor ricocheted around the room: "What? She's in the room?

I thought I caught a whiff of her. Do we need to fumigate the place?"

"Nah. I think she took a shower."

"Then she needs another."

"Shit, we'll have to replace that shower stall."

"Can't, no money in the budget for us."

"Why isn't she in quarantine?"

"I thought hazmat was called in?"

"Shut up, I'm trying to write."

That frustrated yell surprised everyone. One by one, each deputy got back to writing, except those who couldn't get past their writer's block.

"And that completes my dumpster diving duty for the year," Edie said to no one in particular, yet meant for everyone within range of her voice. "Whose turn is it next?"

A chorus of "not me" echoed through the room. And someone yelled, "George, he's not here."

"He shouldn't have taken vacation, if he didn't want the opportunity."

"Who is George? Never heard of him."

"The guy on vacation. The next dumpster diver."

"Heard anything about the boy who was killed?" Edie threw the question out to the room.

"Not much," Steve replied. "It's too early for the autopsy and blood tests to be back. Heard that he's a local boy. Haven't heard if he had a record."

"Any thoughts?" asked Edie.

"This ain't over yet. With two young men gunned down in the last week and no arrests in sight—we're in for a bumpy ride," was Steve's professional opinion.

Other advice was shouted out by other deputies: hang onto our butts, take vacation...now, lock your doors, don't answer the phone, change your name, look for another job, my kids are sick. Anything and everything was shouted to ease the mounting tension in the room. The deputies knew that two bad things had happened, and were anticipating the third, but whether the next bad thing would create a ripple or a tsunami throughout the city or when it would happen wasn't clear.

Then someone shouted the regular August complaint, "Winter can't come too soon." Every cop agreed with that.

Chapter 3

†

Edie kept her car running but put it in park, punched the radio scan button, and leaned back in the seat. In this traffic, she was going nowhere fast. The highway had morphed into a parking lot and she was in the middle of it. She'd forgotten that this was the Sweet Corn Festival weekend in Sun Prairie. If people weren't heading north for entertainment, they'd be heading to Sun Prairie. It looked as if everyone in Dane County was headed to Angel Park for the festival.

After the car behind her honked, again, Edie looked around. What was that driver's hurry? The car in front was now only a half-car length in front of her. Then she looked left; the traffic on Highway 151 was moving fast and had increased. The weekend exodus from Madison and its 'burbs to the Northwoods was nearing its peak. This could be her last chance to join it. Edie imagined herself camping on Madeline Island, the next campers hidden from view, a breeze from Lake Superior blowing through the trees. A haven from August.

The car behind her honked, again. Edie made a decision, put her car in drive, and moved forward onto the Sun Prairie exit ramp. Northern Wisconsin would have to wait. She'd enjoy her days off at her house on the edge of Troutbeck with the wind blowing from the Arlington Prairie, hot and humid as it came across the acres and acres of cornfields.

After dropping her clothes at the cleaner, Edie's thoughts were focused on the best way to get home, until she looked in the rearview mirror. The woman from the dry cleaner was walking toward her car and holding the bag of clothes Edie had just left. Edie gunned it out of the parking lot, wedging her car into the lineup. The cleaners had accepted her bag of clothes. Those clothes were now their problem—she had the ticket to prove it. The drivers had no choice but to let her into the line. Car horns blasted all over the place. What the hell, she thought. If they only knew what she was running from, they'd be more sympathetic and open up a space with no questions asked. Now all she had to worry about was getting out of the standstill traffic.

A left turn at the next lights and Edie could

start planning her three days off. It would begin with a shower, she'd dress in shorts and T-shirt, sit out back under the trees, sip a glass of Vinho Verde or Prairie Fume, whatever was available, and watch Hillary splash in the kiddie pool or maybe watch Breitenbach's corn grow. Three days off, family time, and a glass of wine—life was good.

When Edie pulled into her driveway, Phil waved to her but stayed close to Hillary as she crawled around the front yard. It looked as if those two were doing a good job of entertaining themselves. Her plans for the weekend were falling into place nicely. She put the car into park, turned it off, and leaned back in the seat; could anything be better than a summer's day with friends and family?

The day finally caught up with Edie. A quick catnap in the car would take the edge off. As she shifted to a comfortable position, she accidentally hit the car horn. Phil turned around, picked up Hillary, and walked to the car. He knocked on the window.

Edie rolled it down.

Phil took a step back. "Something die in there?"

"No, it was a bad day at the office. Give me a moment to relax, then I'll open all the windows and air the car out tonight so I can clean it tomorrow. How was your day?"

"Frustrating, that new kid I hired is driving me nuts. I gotta get out of this place. I need to go somewhere I don't have to make big decisions."

"Not me. All I want is a shower, a glass of wine, and the door shut between me and the world."

"I was hoping for a family night at the Sweet Corn Fest."

"Think again, there's lots of stop-and-start crawl traffic in Sun Prairie. I just got out of that mess. I don't want to go back."

"Please, Edie. I need to get lost in a crowd and not solve anyone else's problems."

"Same here. I was thinking of not solving anyone's problems in my backyard. My solution would be less crowded."

"The fest is great."

"I wouldn't know, never been to it."

"What! That seals the deal. We are going. You have to experience it. How could you not have gone to the Sweet Corn Festival? It's the biggest thing this side of Madison during summer. My family went there all the time. We had lots of fun. Best sweet corn ever cooked. Come on, Edie, you'll enjoy it. I can show both my girls a good time."

"I'm not a girl."

"Edie, pleeease."

Edie took a deep breath, let it out slowly. Phil rarely begged. She said yes. "Okay, but I get my shower first."

Chapter 4

†

Edie was nodding off by the time Phil got to the corner store, yet Phil didn't stop talking about his day and Max, the worst driver he ever hired. That kid couldn't find his way out of a shoebox, kept turning off the GPS because he said that he didn't want another woman telling him what to do—he had one mother and that was enough. Edie didn't hear anything else, and later, couldn't remember anything of Phil's rambling speech.

At some point the car stopped moving, the engine was turned off, and Edie felt someone poking her.

"Edie, wake up. Edie. Edie."

"Poke me again and you'll wish you hadn't." The poking stopped, but the whispering didn't. "Shut up," Edie instructed. "I'm awake. Give my eyelids a chance to adjust to this unwelcome reality."

"Come on, Edie, we've been here for five minutes already," said Phil.

"Good, you take the baby. Wake me when you get back," said Edie, releasing her seat belt and reclining the seat. "Do you have a pillow in this car?"

"I've set our wedding day."

"What?" Edie sat up, rubbed her eyes. "Damn, it's still daylight. What did you say?"

"Thought that would get your attention. Come on, let's go. Hillary's first Sweet Corn Fest. This is going to be fun." Phil was putting Hillary in the backpack carrier. He secured her in the pack, lifted it onto his back, and opened the door for Edie. "Come on, the first step is always the hardest."

"You owe me," said Edie, pushing herself out of the car. She stood up and looked around, people were everywhere. There were families with little children, teens in groups, couples, young and old, holding hands, and old people leaning on their canes were walking through the rows of cars toward the midway. They all seemed to have a smile on their face, but that wasn't a good enough reason for her to join them. She closed the door behind her and followed Phil and Hillary toward the midway. "Big time, you owe me big time for this, Phil. Big time," she said when she caught up to them.

Edie and Phil munched on brats during their

second walk through the midway. "I don't see much here for Hillary to eat or do. I think she's a little young for this. Let's go home," said Edie.

"What do you mean? There's the ducky game, the ring toss, spin the wheel, the shooting game...."

"She can't play any of those games by herself. Did we come for you or Hillary?"

"Hillary. I want her to enjoy this as much as I did. Now, tell the truth, isn't this great?"

A man bumped Edie's arm and the lid on her cup came off, spilling pop over her hand. She wiped it off on her shorts. "Not really, it's reminding me of my dumpster dive this morning. Did I tell you about that?"

"Didn't have to, I smelled it. Besides, Edie, it's just pop, it'll wash off. How about dessert? What do you want? I can get you caramel corn, a funnel cake, mini-donuts, caramel apple, snow cone, cotton candy. Cotton candy! Let's get that, Hillary can have some."

"No, she can't."

"Why not?"

"She can't handle that much sugar."

"It isn't all for her, I was going to share it with her."

"Give that girl a taste of cotton candy, she'll grab for the rest, then cry when she can't have any more."

"Fine, I won't give her any, but next year."

"I think this might be a great father-daughter activity for next year."

Edie took pictures of Hillary and Phil picking duckies out of the pond and texted them to Aunt Jill. The smile on Hillary's face when she was handed the prize of a small stuffed dog was Edie's reward for coming—maybe she would come again. "Careful there, King Midas," Edie said as Phil opened his wallet to play the game again.

"What's the problem?"

"We've got another sixteen years of finding places to put her trophies."

"We keep winning like this, I'll build on another room."

"One proud papa."

"Sure am, just like that family over there."

"Which one?"

"Over there, on the other side of the midway, near the fun house. The family having a group hug," said Phil, turning back to the game to hand more of his money to the carnie.

With lots of families, and couples, and groups of teens milling around on the midway, it took Edie a moment to spot the family Phil had mentioned. Did he mean the threesome with their backs toward Edie? The one where the father was holding the woman's hand and his arm was around the girl's shoulder? Edie focused her attention on that family. Something was familiar about them. As she waited for her brain to click on a memory, she saw the girl inch away from her father. Her father tightened his grip on her shoulder, pulled her closer, slid his hand down her hair until it hovered where the girl's hair skimmed the top her butt. Then his hand slipped farther. The girl stepped away. The father's arm went to the girl's waist and pulled her back, then slid to her hips.

"No," Edie demanded. "I know her."

"What?" asked Phil, his attention pulled away from Hillary and the duck game.

"You've got Hillary, right?" Edie didn't wait for a reply. "Catch you later," she said, heading toward the fun house. Elbowing people aside, she made a straight path to the family of three. "Sage?"

The girl turned around. Her father released her. Sage stepped away from him. "Edie! What are you doing here?"

"We're showing Hillary her first carnival. How about you?" asked Edie.

"Sage, remember your manners," her mother interrupted.

"Sorry. Edie, these are my parents," said Sage. "And this is Edie Swift. She lives near Matilda. She's a detective with—"

Edie stepped in. "I'm a detective with the Dane County Sheriff's Office. Nice to meet you two.

21

Good kid you got here. Sage and Matilda babysit for me occasionally; my daughter enjoys spending time with her."

"You're that Edie. Hatch, this is Lisa's neighbor. Nice to finally meet you, Sage has told us a lot about you. Is Mr. Swift with you?"

"There is no Mr. Swift, Phil goes by his own last name," said Edie.

"Oh, you're that kind of woman," said Hatch Staley.

So you're that kind of man, thought Edie. She ignored the challenge and kept the conversation on a superficial level as she assessed Sage's father. "Are you up for the weekend?"

"No. The wife and I are heading back home tonight. Sage will be spending a few days with her Aunt Lisa. So, if you will excuse us, we need to keep moving if we want to take in all of this carnival. Nice meeting you." He held out his hand to Edie. When she took it, he leaned in and whispered, "Detective, you should smile more, you'd be prettier." Hatch Staley took his wife's hand, then walked away.

Edie stepped in front of Sage. "Are you okay?"

Hatch Staley and wife walked a few more feet before realizing that Sage was not with them. Staley turned and called to his daughter, "Sage, are you coming?"

Sage flashed a smiled at Edie and hurried to

catch up with her parents. She stayed two steps behind them.

Edie focused her attention on Sage and didn't notice that someone had stopped behind her.

"Here with the family?" asked Mark Uselman, Madison reporter, leaning over Edie's shoulder.

"That's not my family," replied Edie, still watching Sage and her family until they disappeared into the crowd.

"What's wrong with that family?" Mark asked, following Edie's gaze.

Edie turned to face Mark. The look he got from Edie shut Mark up—fast.

"What are you doing here, Uselman? Trolling?"

"No. I was looking for a place where people seem to be enjoying themselves, not shooting at each other. Seriously, Edie, I come here every year."

"This is my first time here."

"Really! This is your first time at one of the premier events this side of Dane County?"

"Yes, Uselman, really. Why is it so hard for people to believe that?"

"Why are you so defensive?"

"Aunt Jill and I didn't have much money, but we had Madison. What more did we need?"

"When you put it that way, not much. I guess the world does come to the city."

"If you're here to reminisce, why not join Phil and me? The two of you can talk about the olden days at this festival."

"Thanks, I'll pass on the family time. I'll be talking about the old days with some friends over at the beer tent."

Edie caught up with Phil and Hillary at the merry-go-round. "What's that blue stuff around Hillary's mouth?"

"That's between father and daughter," said Phil.

"I'm not stupid. I can see what it is. There is a reason I got to be a detective," said Edie. "I'll confirm my suspicions too. Give me a kiss, little one."

Mother and daughter exchanged a kiss.

"Raspberry or blue moon?" asked Edie.

"My lips are sealed," said Phil.

"Hillary's aren't. She may not be able to tell me what she ate, but the color around her mouth speaks volumes, plus her tongue is blue, and her breath is very sweet smelling."

"Who was the family you were talking to?" asked Phil, attempting to redirect the conversation.

"Sage and her parents."

"Our babysitter Sage?"

"Yes."

"Looks like a nice family."

"Were we looking at the same family?" asked Edie.

Chapter 5

†

Edie thought she could avoid the heat and humidity by taking an early-morning run. She was wrong. She was drenched with sweat by the time she made it to the empty corner store. Edie jogged in place while she reviewed her options of the best route to run. Turn right into farm country with cornfields lining both side and no hint of a breeze to help keep her cool or turn left, which would take her through the tree-lined streets, all two of them, of Troutbeck? As she wiped the sweat from her eyes she noticed the sold sign in front of the store. When had that happened? Edie shook her head in disbelief; that place had been for sale as long as she had lived in Troutbeck. That decided it—a jog through Troutbeck and she might find someone awake who could tell her about it.

The maples, oaks, and the lone surviving elm

tree in the burg provided shade for Edie's jog, but not enough. It didn't look as if anyone was awake, and she didn't see anyone outside their houses, Edie cut her run short. Maybe a night run would be better or a fast walk until the weather broke. She walked back home through the sleeping town.

It took Edie a moment to realize someone was calling her name. She looked to her left and saw Lisa VandenHuevel walking toward her.

"Edie, Edie," Lisa called out.

Edie stopped, reminded herself to put on her poker face, then turned back to meet Lisa. Between Lisa's controlled baby steps and Edie's stride, they met at the end of the VandenHuevels' driveway.

"I am so glad I saw you jogging this morning, I need to talk to you."

"What can I do for you, Lisa?"

"Well, the girls tell me they are going stargazing with you tonight."

"True, Matilda's going to give us a few astronomy lessons."

"Oh good, I didn't know what I was going to do with Sage while she stayed with us. Her mother says Sage has become boy crazy this summer. Lindsey says that when a boy calls, Sage is out the door in a second. I don't know how I'm going to control her. I'm so glad the girls will be with you tonight. I feel so much better that you will be watching over them. I can't think of how I'm going to keep her busy the other days."

"Matilda and Sage seemed to have kept themselves busy in the past, and I don't think you have much boy trouble to worry about in Troutbeck."

"Really, you think so? Why?"

"Are there any boys her age in Troutbeck?"

"Just a few boys on nearby farms."

"Are they hanging around your house?"

"No."

"Then you probably don't have much to worry about, especially with Matilda and Sage pretty much confined to Troutbeck."

"But that's the thing—they both can drive, and Sage has a car here."

"Take away her car keys."

"I can do that?"

"You're responsible for her, aren't you?"

"Yes, but what am I going to do with those girls the rest of the week?"

Edie hoped she didn't sound exasperated. "I'll see if Aunt Jill would like a breather from watching Hillary for a few days. Would that help?"

"Tremendously. Thank-you, thank-you, thank-you."

Edie headed for home. At Sera's house, she turned around and thought about going back to the VandenHuevels'—maybe Lisa could tell her about the store. Then again, she thought, it'll be the talk of the town real soon. Carole will tell me the whole story. Edie went home.

Chapter 6

†

It was dusk and Matilda and Sage still weren't at Edie's house. That left Edie sitting on the porch waiting, thinking about nothing in particular. She kept herself occupied by watching the bats swoop and bank through the growing darkness, chasing mosquitos and other insects that loved the hot, muggy night. She jumped as cold air hit her back.

"Sorry, didn't mean to startle you," said Phil. "You forgot this." He held out Edie's cell phone.

"I won't need that. You keep it. We'll just be over in Breitenbach's field next to us."

"You never know when you'll need it. The light may come in handy."

"No, thanks. I'm taking a vacation from the outside world this weekend; besides, I don't have a good place to put it. I'd probably lose it in Breitenbach's hayfield anyway."

Phil put her phone into his pocket; he was learning when to stop arguing with Edie. "The house is air-conditioned, why not wait for the girls in there?"

"Don't want the girls to ring the doorbell and wake Hillary. So I'm sitting here and watching the bats until Matilda and Sage get here, care to join me?"

"Move over and I'll wait with you."

Edie scooted over a bit.

"What are you thinking about?" asked Phil, breaking the silence.

"It's too hot to think."

"Something must be going on in that brain of yours."

"Watching the bats chase insects and imagining how a screened porch would look here."

Phil launched into more detail about putting in a porch than Edie really wanted to know, but she didn't interrupt his planning; he needed to control something—it sounded like his problems with his business were getting out of hand.

"Our house has a wrong roof line for a porch out front, but maybe I could pour a concrete slab from here to the corner of the house, angle it off at that point, and put in a screened-in gazebo. Why do you want one? Thinking of taking over Harold's job?"

"Keep the mosquitos from eating us alive. As for Harold's job, I don't think anyone wants to take it over. Unless the preacher does—that's right up his alley, keeping everyone on the straight and narrow—not mine. Besides, we're on the wrong end of town to see who gets caught in the speed traps. You know that only farmers come past here, and they drive slowly so they can eye up the crops. How's the new kid working out?"

"Max?"

"That's the one."

"I told you about him last night, but you probably weren't listening."

"When did you tell me?"

"In the car, you might have been sleeping."

"Refresh me; my mental osmosis must not have been working at the time."

"He may be the first person I have to fire—ever."

"The first ever? That's hard to believe. Why fire him?"

"I'm getting complaints about his late pick-ups and deliveries. Can't believe that I hired a kid with no sense of directions."

"Is the GPS unit in his truck working?"

"Yup. Won't follow that, I don't think he turns it on."

"Got a replacement for him lined up?"

"Nope. If I fire him, I'll have to take over his route until I find someone. That may take some time, there's more trucking jobs than drivers these days."

"More long hours for you?"

"Yup, I'm the boss, the shit stops here."

"Thought that was the buck."

"No, that rarely stays around, just keeps going out."

The heat sapped Edie and Phil of more deep conversation; they sat side by side on their porch and watched the bats' acrobatic performances until Matilda and Sage were standing in front of them.

"Hi, Matilda, Sage," said Phil. "Sage, isn't it kind of warm to be wearing that cap?"

Sage ignored him.

"Hi, Mr. Best. You ready, Edie?" asked Matilda.

"Got everything you told me to bring: tarp, sleeping bag, and pillow. I'm ready to do some stargazing. Matilda, I don't understand why we need a sleeping bag in this heat."

"Mosquito protection," said Matilda.

"But it's hot tonight. Won't insect repellent be enough?" asked Edie.

"Do what you want, but I'll be crawling into my sleeping bag to keep the mosquitos away," said Matilda.

"Hi, Sage," Phil said again.

Sage said nothing.

"Cat got your tongue tonight, Sage?"

"No, she's tired of talking to adults," said Matilda, acting as Sage's mouthpiece.

"No, I'm not. I'm tired of them yelling at me and not listening to me. If I don't speak, they'll forget I'm around and leave me alone," said Sage.

"Is that why you're wearing that watchman's cap? Keep from hearing people?" asked Edie.

Matilda elbowed Sage. Sage took two giant steps away from her.

"Take the cap off, show them why you're wearing it," said Matilda.

"Leave me alone, you're just like your mother. It's my hair," shouted Sage.

"I am not. You take that back. I am not like my mother," Matilda shouted back.

Edie and Phil stared from Matilda to Sage hoping one of them would explain what the fight was about.

Matilda stopped glaring at Sage long enough to give them one. "She cut her hair."

"That beautiful hair?" said Phil.

"It's my hair," Sage yelled at him.

"My mother's been yelling at her ever since she cut it this morning," said Matilda.

That must have happened after I talked to Lisa, thought Edie.

"I can do what I want with *my* hair," said Sage.

"Sure, but your parents are really going to go off the deep end when they see it," said Matilda.

"Again, *my hair*. They have nothing to say about it," Sage shot back.

"Let's call this shouting match a draw. Matilda, you promised me shooting stars tonight. Let's go find them," said Edie.

"Well... there might not be many, if any. It is the tail end of the Perseid showers," said Matilda.

"I'll take what I can get. Lead the way," said Edie.

"How about a cell phone?" said Phil.

"Keep it. Yell, if you need me."

Edie lay between Matilda and Sage as they stared at the night sky.

"I don't see any falling stars," said Sage.

"I don't see any either. I see fireflies. I heard an owl. And the coyotes are singing a lot tonight," said Edie.

"Are they close? Maybe we should go home," suggested Sage, inching closer to Edie.

"Don't worry, Sage, those coyotes are a few miles away. Let's keep look for shooting stars. Give your eyes some time to adjust to the night light. They need something like maybe ten to fifteen minutes before you can see much of anything at night. Give it some more time," said Matilda.

"Great, what are we supposed to do until then?" asked Sage.

"Talk," replied Matilda.

"You keep my hair out of it," said Sage.

"Can't. Your hair was beautiful. Your parents loved it. Why'd you cut it?" said Matilda.

"It's my hair, Mattie. I get to decide what I do with it," shouted Sage.

"But your parents..." Matilda started to say.

"Fuck my parents," said Sage.

That silenced everyone for a few moments, Sage never swore.

"They're good parents," whispered Matilda.

"Yeah, if you say so," said Sage.

"Let me see this new hairdo," said Edie, deciding it was time to deescalate the war between the cousins.

"Can't, Matilda wants us to stare at the sky," said Sage.

"I'll chance not seeing a shooting star in the next few minutes or tonight," said Edie. "I'll catch one next year. I understand we pass through these showers once a year. Am I right, Matilda?"

"Once a year," confirmed Matilda.

Edie sat up. "Well, Sage, let me see what all the fuss is about."

Sage stared at the night sky and pulled off the watchman's cap she had been wearing most of the day.

"Sage, sit up. I want to see your whole head," said Edie.

Sage sat up, then ran her hand through the uneven stubble.

"Decent try, but it looks like an amateur chop job. Why haven't you been down to Carole Rhyme's to get it evened off?" asked Edie.

"Sage doesn't have time or money. My mother's been yelling at her almost all day, and didn't mention going to Carole's," said Matilda.

"I don't want to waste my money on a haircut. I've got plans for it," said Sage.

"You need some help with that hair. Go see Carole tomorrow, tell her to put it on my tab," said Edie, remembering the years when she hoped that someone would offer such a simple kindness. Aunt Jill saved money by cutting her hair, and then Edie would spend the next hour trying to even it off.

"You mean that?" said Sage. "You'll pay to get my hair cut?"

"Yes. You can't wear that cap forever, you'll get heat stroke in this weather or worse," said Edie, who then lay down and stared at the sky.

"Wouldn't my parents like that, me getting heat stroke," said Sage. "They wouldn't have to worry about my hair or me."

"I wouldn't like it," said Matilda.

"You may be the only one," whispered Sage.

"I wouldn't like that either, Sage. Matilda, tell me about these shooting stars we're looking for," said Edie, trying to focus the girls' attention on something besides each other and Sage's awful haircut.

Matilda lay down. "Well, you know that shooting stars are really meteors; these ones are part of the Swift-Tuttle comet. The shooting stars are usually visible from mid-July through mid-August. The best time to see a lot of them is over, but maybe we'll see a few tonight."

"Where am I supposed to look?" asked Edie.

"Okay," said Matilda, using a hand as a pointer to direct their attention. "Look north, then to the east a bit. You do know your directions, don't you, Edie?"

"Yes," said Edie, suppressing a chuckle. "I've seen sunrises and sunsets, haven't heard that those have changed directions."

"Sorry, but lots of people don't know that the sun rises in the east and sets in the west. And if you don't know that, how can you find north and south?" said Matilda.

"There's a lot of things I can't figure out about people. You just added one more. Where do I look next?" asked Edie.

"Now look for the constellation which looks like an elongated W or M—that's Cassiopeia. Once you've spotted it, look to the north of the whacky-looking leg, that's where the Perseus constellation is. And that is where we can see the focal point of the meteor showers."

"What's a focal point?" asked Sage.

"That's where the meteors will come from," Matilda answered.

"Okay, I see the W," said Edie.

"Edie, are you really going to pay for my haircut?" asked Sage.

"Yes, I'll text Carole right now," said Edie, searching her pockets for her cell. "Sorry, I guess I left my cell at home. I'll text her when I get back home."

Edie spotted a shooting star and followed it until it blazed out, and then turned her gaze back to Perseus to look for another, but something was blocking the stars. It was Phil. "Move, please, you're blocking my view."

Phil handed Edie her cell. "You need to call the office. It sounded real important."

Edie noted Phil's look of concern as she took the phone from him.

"No. You gotta text Carole," shouted Sage, sitting up.

Edie glanced at Sage and sent a text to Carole to expect Sage tomorrow. "Done. Now it's up to you, Sage, to follow through." When Edie saw the callback number, she shoved the phone into a pocket, then started to gather her stuff. "Girls, I've got to leave. I think you two should head home."

"Why? I want to stay, I'm seeing more shooting stars than I thought would be out," said Matilda.

"Maybe we can do this again tomorrow night," said Edie. "But tonight I would be happier if you two went home." She waited for Matilda and Sage to gather their stargazing gear. Then she and Phil followed them out of Breitenbach's hayfield. Edie stopped at her house and watched as the girls headed home. Matilda put an arm around Sage, and Sage reciprocated; soon, the two heads were touching and it looked as if the two of them were talking.

"How'd the night go?" asked Phil when Edie finally went in.

"Decent, I saw some shooting stars and prevented another cousins' war. Why'd you leave our baby alone?"

"You didn't take your phone. And you needed to return that call. Besides, we were only yards away, nothing to worry about in Troutbeck."

"I'm beginning to doubt that," said Edie.

Chapter 7

†

Edie listened and nodded during the phone call she made into the department, ending the listening session with, "I'll be in." She sat for a moment after hanging up, took a deep breath in, let it out slowly, and pushed off the couch.

"What's going on?" asked Phil.

"Trouble in Madison. Protesting erupting across Madison. A curfew has been issued and the Madison PD asked for mutual aid to help enforce it. I knew I should've turned the phone off—we could've spent the weekend in ignorant bliss."

"What happened?"

"Drive-by shooting. A little kid's in the hospital. Groups of people taking over the streets. Vandalism. Damn. We've been waiting for something like this to happen. It's anyone's guess as to how bad this will get."

"Do you have to go?"

"Yes."

"Why?"

Disbelief spread over Edie's face. "It's my job, I'm a cop."

"But it's your weekend off."

"Doesn't matter. The Madison PD needs all the help they can get."

"But what about us? You've got a baby in the next room. What if..." Phil choked and started again. "The thing is everyone hates cops these days—you've got a target on your back."

"I'll be wearing my vest."

"That's not going to stop people from shooting at you."

"No, it won't, but it may save my life."

"It's only a vest. It doesn't cover your whole body."

"I know. I'll just have to stay more alert." Edie waited for Phil to ask the next unthinkable and unanswerable question. It took its time in coming.

"What if you don't make it back?"

"I will."

"How many cops have said that to their families and then they never came back?"

"I don't know." Edie paused for a moment. What was Phil trying to tell her? "You scared?"

"Every time you go work."

"There's nothing left for me to say, Phil. I'm

not quitting my job. You knew what I did for a living when you kept asking me out. You've got to come to terms with this by yourself. I have, that's why I insisted that we have a will. That's why I don't hog all of Hillary's time, though I'd like to. I'd love to have a heart-to-heart with you right now, but I gotta go."

"You're not the savior of the world, you know."

"No, I am not. This is just me doing the job I signed on for. You probably won't like hearing this, but you're not my whole life, only one part of it." Edie hesitated for a moment. She felt like she was looking into the void, then finished her thoughts. "Phil...if the unthinkable happens, find a good woman to marry and look after you and Hillary."

"Sounds like my mother's plan. Not mine."

"Good, I didn't want to come back and haunt you. What's your plan?"

"Find the woman I love, marry her, then live happily ever after."

"Have you found her?"

"I have, but she won't marry me."

"That discussion is for another time. I gotta go. If you need help, call Aunt Jill, or Carole, or maybe Matilda and Sage—Lisa would appreciate that."

Edie made the opening, Phil took it. "What about our daughter? Where does Hillary fit into your life?"

That brought Edie up short. She let go of the

door handle, then stepped back toward Phil. "She is my heart. I have to go, I've work to do." Edie turned away from Phil. A second later she turned back to face him. "When I am not here...." The thought of never again being with Hillary and Phil shut Edie up for a bit until she gained control of herself again. "When I am not here I have entrusted her to you and Aunt Jill."

There seemed to be a widening rift between Edie and Phil, and Phil reached across it. "Me, too." Phil stood in front of the door and gave Edie a hug and a lingering kiss. "Take care; I don't think I can find another you." And then he stepped aside.

"Sounds like a song, but you don't have to sing it for me now."

Edie sat in her car, wiped away the tears, and backed her car out of the driveway. She noticed that the dumpster odor in her car still lingered. Didn't matter, she'd have to live with it; there wasn't time to clean it. Edie pushed the radio scan button looking for something soothing. The radio scanned through hard rock, folk protest songs, 1960s protest songs, rap songs, but when it blasted the local news, Edie punched it off. She didn't want to hear any news updates as she drove into Madison. Soon enough she'd be in the middle of its craziness.

It was a quiet ride to the city's edge, and the deeper she went into the city the quieter it got. Streets were empty. Houses looked closed up. The city looked and felt as if it had been abandoned. It reminded Edie of the way the city looked and felt during a tornado warning. She was sorry for the people nailing themselves into their houses; there was no way of telling how many people had air-conditioning. She hoped they all did. But she knew from her patrolling days there were a lot of older homes in Madison that had not been upgraded. There was no way that any resident was prepared for the recently imposed curfew. They could prepare for blizzards, but never a curfew. Being cooped up in this heat and humidity might cause people to break the curfew.

The closer she got to central Madison, the more Edie felt the weight of something, as if that something was hovering over the city. It was oppressive. She could feel it begin to ooze through the empty streets. Maybe it was sweat-infused with fear that had dripped from each person and had escaped from the houses and into the street. Edie couldn't put her finger on it. Hidden beneath the city's silence, something was lying in wait, for what she didn't know. Would the curfew be able to contain it?

As she neared the first outer ring of streets

around the Capitol, Edie saw police squads fanning out into her Madison. She wondered if the curfew could hold.

Chapter 8

†

Edie got the short form of the report: in response to scattered outbreaks of violence, Madison had imposed a curfew—no one on the streets. At this point, the sergeant told the deputies to listen up, because this was really important—Monona, Middleton, Fitchburg, Town of Madison, and Shorewood Hills also had curfews, and no one was happy about it. There was a collective sigh of relief from the officers in the briefing room; they no longer had to remember where one municipality ended and the next began.

While waiting for her assignment, Edie got the details of the situation from her fellow deputies. A drive-by shooting, target missed but a toddler took the bullet—collateral damage that seemed to be the trigger for the outbreaks. In one area vandalism and looting were occurring. Another, people were pouring into the streets to protest—anger over the slow response of the police to recent shootings, anger over racial profiling during traffic stops, anger that there were too many guns and no one was doing a damn thing about it, and anger about whatever was left in their lives to be angry about. Just one big explosion of anger. In another part of the city, streets were being blocked off. Rumor was that no one would be patrolling alone until the streets were really quiet. She hoped for an experienced deputy.

Edie barely heard the stories being told around. My poor Madison, Edie thought. When had her city changed? She'd heard that people used to feel safe enough to sleep outside on hot summer nights. That probably couldn't happen these days. Hard for her to believe that Madison, with its beautiful lakes, wonderful bike paths, and a world-class university, a mini-paradise, was not immune from the world's troubles.

Edie was partnered with one of the twins— Deputy Garth Smith. No one would be patrolling alone until the streets of Madison were really quiet.

Edie got their assigned area for the next few days or however long it took—southeast side of Madison and the adjacent parts of Monona. She put on her bulletproof vest, secured a body cam, and then met up with Smith. They decided on a coin toss to see who got to drive. Smith fished a quarter from his pocket and tossed it.

"Tails," Edie called. She waited for the coin to land. "When did children become collateral damage?"

"Beats me," said Smith, catching the coin and flipping it onto the back of his hand. "Heads. You lose."

The ride to their assigned patrol area was quiet and uncomfortable. Edie knew next to nothing about Smith; sure, they had worked together a few times, but only enough to exchange hellos and work gossip. She wondered what they were going to talk about during the hours that stretched until dawn. Mentally she compiled a list of topics. There was no need to do that. It seemed as if Smith had something to get off his chest.

"My wife's freaked out about what's happening. She says I'm a sitting duck these days. That maybe I should quit and get a different job. Some days I agree with her, but all in all, I like this job," said Smith.

"Phil's been saying the same thing," said Edie. "I didn't know you were married." She didn't add that she thought him and Johnson were yoked together in adolescence forever and would never commit to anything. Just goes to show, you never can tell, she thought.

"Jumped into it a few years back. Had to."

This shocked Edie. "Getting pregnant doesn't have to lead to shotgun weddings anymore."

"What? We didn't get married because she was pregnant. We are only just pregnant with our first kid."

"Congratulations. Since she wasn't pregnant, then why did you get married?"

"Her hours were cut, she lost her benefits. She needed health insurance. We'd talked about getting married before that happened, but the loss of benefits pushed us into marriage."

"Regret the decision?"

"No, should've done it earlier. What about you?"

"I can't think of any reason to get married."

"I read somewhere that married couples live longer."

"I thought that advantage went to men, what do women get out of it?"

"Lawn mowing, getting stuff fixed around the house, heavy lifting."

"Did all that when I was young, and do it now, too."

"How'd you learn those skills, from your father?"

"My father was never on the scene. I did it

out of necessity. It was only my Aunt Jill and me. Got a book on home repairs and maintenance out of the library and read it. Give me another reason to get married."

"Let me think...I remember that you got a kid, so free babysitters—you get free babysitters. I'm sure my mother-in-law will be camping out at our house soon waiting for the birth of her grandbaby. These days if my wife even thinks about the baby, it seems as if her mother calls. I think I can handle my mother-in-law being at our house to help with the baby; don't know what I'll do if she decides to move in permanently."

"True, but I already got free sitters. And there aren't any telepathic messages being sent between Phil's mother and me about us needing babysitters. We're not BFFs."

"Too bad."

"Isn't it. Got anything else?"

"Only adolescent boy chatter that's better left on the playground or in the locker room."

Tapped out of things to discuss, Edie and Smith concentrated on the quiet streets they were patrolling and the darkness between the streetlights.

"This isn't the Madison I remember," said Smith.

"Me neither. I remember friendly neighborhoods, a small college town. When I was at the university, I remember the out-of-state students saying how friendly the town was. I wonder if they still say that. How did we get to here? When did Madison forget who we are?" said Edie.

"Stop, soon I'll be contemplating my navel and running this car up a light pole. Don't know about you, but I need something to help keep me awake. Let's find a coffee place, looks like it is going to be a long night."

"Think anything will be open?"

"Hope so. If not, I'll call the wife and have her make up a couple of thermoses of coffee, and then I'll swing by my place to pick them up." Smith took the next right. "Looks as if it's all quiet on this street."

"Exactly what I was hoping for."

Smith took another right. At the corner, there was a coffee shop with its lights still on and two police squads parked out front. Smith pulled in next to them. Edie and Smith got out of the squad to order coffee at the window.

Lieutenant Gracie Davis greeted them before they got there. "You made it before closing time."

"Thought this was an all-night joint," said Smith.

"It's closing up soon and won't have night hours until the curfew is lifted," said Gracie. "Hey, Edie."

"Hey, yourself, what are you doing out here?"

"Rendering assistance to someone in need. The kid's here by himself and is a bit scared. Doesn't

want to close the place by himself and doesn't want
to be charged with breaking the curfew on his way
home. So I'm here to escort him home. And doing
my part to contain the stupid."

"Good luck with that part," said Edie.

"What stupid stuff?" asked Smith.

Edie looked away from Smith, he was on his
own. Apparently, no one had clued him that the
stupid topic was one of Gracie's pet peeves. Curb-
ing stupidity among cops was one of her more
infamous lectures. He stepped in it, and she wasn't
going to help him out—he'd learn and remember.
Experience was the best teacher.

"Deputy Smith, you've been through the aca-
demy. There you were taught methods of handling
any situation you might encounter. But we police
are people, too, we experience the same fight-or-
flight response in difficult situations that other
people do. Many people flee, but we don't. We
don't flee. We stay because it is our job to stay.
So, that puts us squarely in the fight mode. But
we're not supposed to be there. The next step we
cops should be taking is figuring out what the real
problem is and how to control. We don't always get
to that next step. Some of us stop along the way and
let weapons, our immediate backup in a fight, do
the controlling instead."

Edie hoped this would be the short version of
the lecture. Hadn't anyone clued Smith in about
Gracie?

"That's when we make stupid mistakes; lives that we have sworn to protect are now in danger. We are better than that." Gracie stopped.

The heat must be getting to Gracie, she gave the short version, thought Edie, and she usually goes on and on. But Gracie wasn't finished.

"Lots of stupid has been on display recently, here and other places in our country. Take your pick of which ones you want to talk about. Tonight in Madison we've got shooting, looting, and mooning," said Gracie.

"Thought that mooning fad went out years ago," said Smith.

"It came back in force tonight. Seems as if the only thing people can do when forced to spend a summer's night inside is to hang their bare asses out the window," said Gracie. "But I'll take bare butts over bullets any day, on condition that they keep those things out of my face."

Smith was quiet. Edie hoped he was memorizing Gracie's sermon because if he didn't, he'd hear it often.

"These quiet streets are giving me the creeps, kind of reminds me of the calm before tornados," said Smith.

"Be glad you're in the calm part of the city. Depending on how long this lasts, you'll get rotated into the hot spots," said Gracie.

"I hope that this time-out cools people off," said Smith.

"Me too, Deputy, me too," said Gracie. "How people will react to being cooped up with this heat is anyone's guess. So to come back to your point, Edie, I'm here to reduce the stupid on our part, so keep your brain open. You too, Smith."

"Hard to avoid stupid in this heat," said Edie.

"And yet we have to, Detective Swift. We have to," said Gracie. "If we can control ourselves, we have a better chance of controlling the situation."

The lecture wasn't over. Should have kept my mouth shut, thought Edie.

"Just like the sheriffs did in the old westerns, they controlled the situation. I used to watch them with my grandparents. *Gunsmoke, The Rifleman, Bonanza.* I can't remember the others," said Smith.

Gracie turned her gaze to Smith. Edie was surprised that Smith wasn't melting under that gaze.

"Guessing you two stopped for coffee. Better place your order now; in a few minutes I'm escorting that boy home," said Gracie.

Edie and Smith placed their order. When they had their order and were out of Gracie's hearing, Smith whispered to Edie, "When did she become a preacher?"

"Always been one since I've known her," Edie whispered back.

Chapter 9

†

Edie and Smith bought two cups of coffee each; they downed the first cup of coffee as they kept their squad to a crawl through their assigned neighborhoods. It was quiet, mercifully quiet—until the radio call came that someone was at the Lowell Elementary School playground. They weren't the only ones responding to the call, lots of lights and sirens were descending on the school. When she and Smith pulled into the playground area, Edie counted two other squads that had pulled in beside them.

Edie did a quick assessment of the situation. Three squads with their headlights illuminating a school playground, and in the fenced-in playground three boys stood frozen in place near the basketball hoops. They're just boys out shooting baskets on a summer's night, thought Edie. Hope this doesn't turn into one of those stupid moments Gracie was talking about.

Edie took over the lead, Smith stayed behind the car door.

"Boys, this is Detective Swift of the Dane County Sheriff's Office. I'm here with other deputies and Madison Police officers. I need you to drop the basketball and your put hands in the air over your head." It took a second request from Edie before the boys understood what she wanted them to do, and what was happening around them. They raised their hands and the basketball bounced away.

Edie was first to reach the boys. They looked young; a steps-and-stairs family of tow-heads and freckles, there didn't appear to be much difference in their ages. The oldest was what, maybe twelve, thirteen years old tops. She got a whiff of strong urine odor coming from the boys, and saw a puddle form under each boy. She suppressed memories of her recent dumpster dive and kept her need to puke under control. "What are you doing outside of your house?"

"Playing basketball," the shortest one said.

Edie heard an unspoken "duh" in there. She ignored it. "Why?"

"We ain't got nothing else to do."

And Madison teachers have their work cut out correcting these boys' English. She refrained from correcting them and stayed on topic. "Do you know that there's a citywide curfew in effect? That means no one on the streets after eight."

"When did that happen?" asked the shortest one.

"This evening," said Edie.

"How were we supposed to know that? We don't have a TV," one boy said.

"You don't have a TV," echoed Edie. Hard to believe these days, she thought. The boy's comment did remind her of Aunt Jill's stories of growing up and televisions were a luxury, but Edie never knew a kid or family that didn't have one.

"Yeah, our folks say we shouldn't waste our time and their money on junk like that. We should be reading or maybe out playing or working in the yard or garden—stuff like that—not baking our brains watching TV."

"Okay," said Edie. "Didn't you boys see that no one else was on the streets? Didn't you wonder why that was?"

"We thought that was kinda weird," said the boy who was speaking for his brothers. "But I don't get to tell my neighbors what to do, only my brothers. Tonight we wanted to shoot some hoops."

"I'll accept that for now," said Edie. "Now, where do you boys live?"

"Across the street," said the boy who had

become the group's spokesperson. He pointed to a house directly across from the playground.

"Are your parents home?"

"No."

"How can we contact them?" asked Edie.

The boys said nothing.

With explosive situations popping up around the city, Edie wasn't going to play twenty questions with any adolescent. "Boys, there is a curfew in place. Everyone is supposed to stay off the streets and inside their homes. We may have to take you to juvenile detention; your parents can pick you up there."

After that, the boys couldn't talk fast enough. One parent, they said, was at work, and the other with friends somewhere. The working parent was called and arrangements made for her to come home.

The other police took notes to refer to later, no telling when they would have the time to write up their report on this incident.

"Could we get our ball back?" the oldest boy asked.

Edie sent Smith to retrieve it.

It was a relief for Edie and the other officers that the boys spilled their guts. It meant less paperwork for them.

Back in the squad, and parked on a side street,

Edie and Smith took turns entering their reports in the Mobile Data Terminal.

"Is this town going crazy?" Smith asked. "Two squads responding to three kids playing basketball."

"Three, you're forgetting us," Edie corrected. "We're all nervous. We don't know when or where the next outbreak of violence will be or what will set it off. So we respond with a show of force."

"If this keeps up, I'll insist that my wife get out of town, go visit her parents or something."

"Chivalrous of you."

"Ain't it. But with her out of town, it'll help me keep my mind on the job instead of worrying about her."

"I live out of town, but know what you're talking about. Been thinking about the family a lot."

Edie and Smith downed their cold cups of coffee, and drove lots of miles before the false dawn glowed on the horizon.

"Any plans when you get off duty?" asked Smith

"Heading for my aunt's house for a long sleep," said Edie.

"Not going home, why?"

"Too tired to drive that far and don't want to run into the ditch or cause an accident. How about you?"

"My plans are to sleep until my wife thinks

I should be doing something else," said Smith. "Christ, I need to take a piss right now. Think anything's open we can stop at?"

"Nope. No one's on the street. We'll find a park, and then you can use a tree."

"That's illegal."

"These are unusual circumstances. I won't write you a ticket, I promise—a pinkie swear or something like that."

"With my luck, somebody would use me for target practice or snap pictures of me to put on the Internet. If any of that happens, I'd become one more story for Ben to tell. I'd never live it down."

"Don't worry, I wouldn't let that happen, I've got your back. Besides, Ben has plenty of cousins to talk about, don't think he needs to tell stories about us."

"He'd probably adopt me postmortem."

"Posthumously," said Edie. "The word is posthumously."

"I'll be dead, use whatever word you want. I just don't want to be one of his stories. Then there's you."

"What? You're shy? You've been telling me your life story all night. What's a little skin between best buds? Besides, once you've seen one dick, you've seen them all."

"I'm willing to wait."

Chapter 10

†

Edie woke to the sound of a loud thump on the floor. It took a moment for her to realize that the thump in the night that she heard was her falling out of bed. She looked around; it was day, she corrected herself—she was the one who went thump in the day. Her brain fog lifted enough for her to remember she was crashing at her aunt's house. She pulled the blanket and pillow off the bed. That bed used to be bigger, she thought. She spread the blanket out, punched the pillow into shape, looked for another pillow to place over her head to block the sunlight, but couldn't find one. She abandoned the search when she remembered she and Aunt Jill could only afford one pillow per bed—it was too much work to get the pillow from her aunt's room. She lay down and put her arm across her face to block out the light. That didn't work. Sleep escaped her. She should be up anyway preparing for her next shift.

Edie sat on the floor, her back against the bed, her knees touching the dresser directly across from the bed, and she took stock of her room while she waited for her brain to kick into gear. Nothing had changed in the room. The bed, which had been her mother's, was still pushed up against the wall under the window. The dresser, a dumpster dive treasure that she and Aunt Jill found during the annual Hippie Christmas, filled the rest of the room. The space between the two pieces of furniture was barely enough to turn around in. Legally the window and door qualified it as a room. These days the room wouldn't be big enough for a walk-in closet. But back in the day, it was all hers—a teeny, tiny sanctuary to escape the world. The room looked as if Aunt Jill had closed the door to this bedroom and never looked back when Edie left home for the university. And during those intervening years, the room had somehow gotten smaller.

Edie rested her chin on her knees and then opened the bottom drawer of the dresser. It was full of her high school stuff. She hadn't emptied it before leaving for the university, and it was apparent that Aunt Jill hadn't touched it either. She took out a shirt and put it on. It was a tight fit in the upper arms; if she hunched her shoulders to get her boobs reduced she was able to button it, for a second. The shirt must have been from when she was a freshman in high school. She'd grown since then. Edie pulled it off, threw it back in the drawer, and shoved the drawer shut. It looked as if neither she nor Aunt Jill wanted to stroll down that memory lane and decide what should be tossed. Someday soon she'd promised herself she would make a point of clearing out her embarrassing adolescent stuff before Hillary found it. She shoved the drawer closed, threw the blanket and pillow back on the bed, and explored the rest of the house.

It was a short trip. Edie could repeat her grandmother's defense that the house had been built as a shelter for a small family during hard times, not a showplace for their money. Through two generations it stayed that way—not a showplace. There were three bedrooms, one an exact replica of the room that had been hers and a third larger bedroom meant for a couple. The bathroom was still painted in Mamie Eisenhower pink—why hadn't Aunt Jill changed that? A living room, an eat-in kitchen, no space for a separate dining room, and a back porch built by her grandfather completed the house. Edie often heard her grandmother say, "It's a roof over your head, be glad you have one." And she was when she went home to Aunt Jill's one-bedroom apartment. And she was really glad to have a roof over her head when she got back from searching for her mother in Florida.

On that trip, she had found her mother—at least her mother's house. Edie sat on the front step waiting for the woman who had given her birth.

It was late afternoon when that woman appeared. It was eerie that she looked a lot like Aunt Jill. Edie hadn't expected that.

The woman stared at Edie. "How'd you get here?"

"Bus."

"What do they call you these days?"

"Edie."

"No they don't. My mother never liked nicknames. What's your real name?"

"Edith's on my birth certificate."

"Moon Shadow is on the first one."

Edie nearly puked. Even Edith was better than Moon Shadow. "I'm Edie. What's yours?"

"Wanda."

Edie knew that, she needed her mother to confirm it.

Wanda stepped up to the front door.

Edie let her pass.

"I suppose you want to come in to pee or something."

Of course she did, but Edie remained silent.

Wanda opened the door, Edie followed her in.

Wanda was in the kitchen when Edie came out of the bathroom.

"I suppose you want something to eat," Wanda said.

"That would be nice."

"There's some peanut butter and bread on the table, help yourself," Wanda said, leaving the kitchen.

Edie did, making two sandwiches.

Wanda returned wearing a sundress and putting in hoop earrings. "Where you spending the night?"

"Here?" Edie was betting against reality. In her mother's house, there was no room or bed for Edie.

"Only one bedroom in this house, and I'm using it tonight. You can't stay here."

"Where am I supposed to go?"

"Got yourself down here by bus, didn't you? You'll find something."

Edie did. The few days she'd spent in Florida were divided by nights wandering on the beach while wondering about her future, sleeping in the back doorway of her mother's house during the day when her mother was gone. Then at night she returned to the beach with a backpack stuffed with food that she scrounged from her mother's house after she forced open a window and crawled in, and a blanket she pulled off the couch before leaving the way she came in. She was just thirteen, wandering the world by herself. After a few nights on her own, she had enough. Someone once told her that if lost, stay put—that wasn't an option. Others said to go back to where you started. With money found in her mother's dresser, Edie bought a bus ticket and returned to Madison.

"Enough of yesterdays," Edie said, running her fingers through her hair as if to remove the cobwebs and shards of those memories. "Enough. I've got to focus on today and I am starving."

There was nothing in the fridge. She found a can of soup, a half-empty box of crackers in the cupboard. Edie munched on a cracker, immediately spitting it out in the wastebasket. It was old and stale. The box of crackers followed. She carefully read the soup can label, it was a year past the best-by date. That followed the crackers into the wastebasket. She began to wonder if Aunt Jill ever stayed in Madison, and what the hell was she feeding Hillary when they spent time at this house? With soup and crackers gone she'd have go out for food.

Edie's first choice of restaurants was the local pancake house. When she drove into the restaurant's parking lot there were loads of parents pushing strollers around the lot, grown sons and daughters helping their parents maneuver walkers across the uneven pavement; it was too much for

Edie. Even though there had been no big problems during last night's patrol, today she wanted to be someplace where other people weren't. She wasn't up for cooking. That would expend more energy and brainpower than she had available. Deli food seemed to be the answer to her hunger.

At the grocery store, Edie studied the coffee selections: blend versus single source, dark roast versus medium versus light, finely ground versus coarse ground versus bean. Too many choices, and her brain refused to make any more decisions. She grabbed an instant coffee jar.

"Fine choice, Detective," said a man standing next to her. "My backup for when I can't get to a coffee stand."

She turned toward him. "Uselman, thought you'd be sleeping off last night's drunk."

"I did. It's afternoon now."

"Why did they let you back into Madison?"

"Couldn't stop me, I live here, and I showed them my press credentials. What are you doing here? Thought this was your weekend off."

"I'm helping to protect the good citizens of Madison and its 'burbs."

"What about the bad ones?"

"Them too. They deserve equal protection, too. Everyone's innocent until proven guilty. What are you doing in the store?"

"Looking for food and a story. Got either?"

"Food—none, that's why I'm here, and I'm still debating how much I want to cook today. If you want stories, talk to the sheriff's public relations officer."

"Was the code of silence decreed also?"

"No, I'm too tired to tell you a story. But if you need one, look around, lots of people here trying to figure out how long the curfew will last and what to stock up on if it lasts longer than a blizzard—go ask them for a story."

Uselman looked up and down the aisle. "See what you mean. Have you made a decision on what you're going to eat?"

"No, maybe you can help. Should I cook at home or take deli?"

"Deli, it saves time. Why isn't Phil cooking for you?"

"I slept in Madison."

"Did you two split or something?"

"I was too tired to drive home, didn't want to get into an accident. So I slept at my aunt's house."

"Good, glad to know that you haven't totally abandoned Madison for country living. How about me keeping you company?"

"Thanks for the offer, but I'm going to eat, then sleep, alone, before going back on duty. Don't have time for company or storytelling."

"Your loss. Get their tomato bisque soup, it is delicious."

Edie put the few groceries she'd purchased in the fridge and her deli food in the microwave. She set it for reheat, stripped off her clothes, threw them in the washing machine, wrapped a towel around herself, then sat down to eat. The tomato bisque soup was good, the croissant acceptable, the chocolate cake with ganache frosting was delicious, and the fruit she'd eat later on patrol. The food tasted better because she didn't have to make it herself. Too bad she'd be back at work that night; a glass or two or three of a Vinho Verde wine would complete the meal nicely. Shit, since she was daydreaming, why not the whole bottle—might as well make it a big dream.

While she ate, thoughts of her grandparents, her mother, and Aunt Jill crowded everything else out. How was it possible for four people to live in this postage stamp-sized house and not drive each other nuts? But they were nuts, except maybe Aunt Jill. No, Aunt Jill didn't get a pass in that department, maybe by degree—she was the least crazy of the four.

How did three women cook in this teeny-tiny kitchen? They didn't, she remembered. According to Aunt Jill, she and her mother left home as soon as possible. Her mother wandered to parts unknown, returning to Madison to give birth to Edie and then leave, again, without her baby. She finally settled down in Florida.

Aunt Jill moved into her own teeny-tiny space down near the university as soon as she could, and returned to this house after her parents were dead, with a growing Edie, whom she somehow inherited, in tow.

Edie's phone dinged, a message from Phil. It was a picture of her baby walking, her first steps alone. Edie brushed aside a tear and called Phil. "Thanks for the picture. When did Hillary start walking?"

"A moment ago. How long have you been off work?"

"Earlier today."

"You couldn't have called?"

"Sorry, but I needed to take care of the basics, such as sleep, hunger, and destressing before the next shift. So I slept at Aunt Jill's 'cause I didn't want to end up in a ditch between Madison and home. Or, worse, getting into a car accident and killing someone. Did you know that Aunt Jill has nothing in her house to eat?"

"Not surprised, she's spending most of her time these days on the farm with Hank. Why don't you come home? I know a few ways to help relax you."

"Did I mention I needed sleep?"

"My mother called."

"Sorry to disappoint her, but you can tell her that I'm still alive."

"I told her that. I'm taking Hillary over there for a few hours. Want me to stop by?"

"Sweet idea, but my plans are different. First, I'm going to take a shower because I can smell myself and it isn't pleasant. Then I'm going back to sleep 'cause it looks like there will be another long night for me. So...for now, I'm focusing on the basics."

"Aren't I one of your basic needs?"

Edie heard the hurt in Phil's voice and jettisoned the snappy comebacks for the direct approach. "Yes, you are." That was all that was needed. For the next minute, the only thing Edie heard was Phil's breathing.

"Are you coming home tonight?" asked Phil.

"Only if this thing blows over here."

"Marry me."

"Why?"

"Our neighbors think we are. We should make it a reality."

"I'm not jumping into their delusions. Hey, don't really want to cut this short, but I feel a nap coming on. Call you later, okay? Love you."

"Love you back."

Edie waited for Phil to hang up. It took a few minutes.

Chapter 11

†

Edie and Smith were together again, same squad, same time, same place, almost a different day.

"Looks like we're going to be best buds for a while," said Smith.

"Sure does. Best buds driving through the night," said Edie.

"Yeah, what do you want to do?"

"Well, since we can't blow this popsicle stand, why don't we cruise the streets to let the good people of Dane County and Madison know we got their backs," said Edie.

"Wish they had ours."

"Most of them do. They're just tired of the recent dumb cops and dead people moments that are popping up across the country."

"I am too, but I wasn't there. And I didn't do that stuff. And I don't know what those cops faced.

They don't know what those cops faced. Why is everyone angry at me? Damn. Do they know how difficult this job's become?"

"Doubt it. Probably hasn't crossed their minds. In their defense, we signed on for this job—not them. Take the next right; we haven't been down that street since last night."

Instead, Smith turned left; nothing had changed since last night either—the street was still quiet, except for the person out walking after curfew.

Smith drove past the person, did a U-ey, followed the curfew breaker for a few feet, turned on the lights, and then pulled up behind her.

Edie, riding shotgun, was the first out of the squad. She turned on her body cam. "Excuse me, ma'am." Edie judged the woman to be about her own height; she was wearing shorts, tank top, and flip-flops.

The woman kept on walking.

"Ma'am, I'm a police officer. I need you to stop. Now."

The woman stopped, turned, and watched as Edie closed the gap between them in a few steps. "Oh, it's you. Can't you find someone else to harass? Who are you going to bother when I'm gone?"

Edie couldn't remember a time when she had harassed Leigh Stone, except that time when they first met. And that didn't count—she was protecting her family. No one was going to take a picture of her child and splash it across TV for everyone's entertainment. How could anyone carry a grudge that long? "Deputy Smith, will you handle this one?" Edie called out.

Smith joined Edie. "Sure. What do we have here?"

"Someone out after curfew, haven't asked her any questions yet." Edie stepped off to one side to let Smith take over.

Smith took over. "Ma'am, may I have your name?"

"Leigh Stone." She continued to glare at Edie. "L-E-I-G-H. Stone, you should be able to handle that one."

"Do you have any ID with you?"

"No. I left it in my apartment."

"Did you know that a curfew is still in effect?"

"Yes."

"Is there a reason you are out after curfew?"

"I needed some fresh air."

"I'm going to cite you for violating curfew," said Smith.

"I resent this harassment. I'm a reporter."

"Are you currently performing the activities related to your job?"

There was a long pause before Stone answered. "No...yes. I was looking for someone to interview about this curfew. All I found were people cursing the police. Tell that to your bosses."

Smith pulled his ticketing book from his pocket. "I will pass that on. Your name again, please."

"Leigh Stone, one pissed-off reporter."

"Your address?"

"My apartment is at the end of this block. We can see it from here."

"Ma'am, I still need your legal address."

"Did she put you up to this?"

"Who are you talking about, ma'am?"

"Your partner. That woman," Leigh Stone said, pointing at Edie. "She needs to be off the streets herself, could probably start a riot all by herself."

"No, my partner did not 'put me up to this'. We both saw someone breaking curfew, we stopped to investigate. May I please have your address?"

It took Leigh Stone some time to conclude it was in her best interest to stop haranguing Smith and give him the information he was asking for. After handing Stone the citation, Edie and Smith escorted her to her apartment.

"Why does that woman have it in for you?" Smith asked when they got back into the squad.

"Imaginary stuff. Hasn't liked me since the Washington case," said Edie.

"I remember that case; it was the first time I was on my own. That's a long time to carry a grudge."

The dispatcher's report stopped their conversation. "Report of people at Esther Beach Park.

Officers on the scene are requesting a female officer presence."

"We got one of those," said Smith. He called back to the dispatcher that he and Edie were responding and that they would be on scene soon. He turned on the lights and sirens, then beelined it down Monona Drive.

There were three other squads at the park when they got to Esther Beach.

"Never been to this beach," said Edie as they pulled into the parking lot.

"Nice-looking little neighborhood park," said Smith. "Didn't know it existed, either. Looks like a nice place to raise a kid or two."

"If you can afford it. Take a look around, it's expensive living on any Madison lake, and the houses around here aren't too shabby."

"Maybe we could swing a small house a few blocks from the lake."

"You keep on dreaming, Smith."

Edie and Smith walked over to the other officers who were standing at the water's edge.

"Look at that view." Smith let out a low whistle.

"That is pretty, I like seeing the Capitol lit. And there's the generating plant. Wonder why it isn't included in pictures of the Madison skyline?" asked Edie.

"Because it's reality, not scenic," said one of the officers standing at the lake's edge.

"Thank God you're here," said another Madison officer, looking at Edie. He turned toward the lake. "Girls, we got a woman cop here. You need to come out of the lake. Now."

"No," yelled the girls in unison, as they moved deeper into Lake Monona.

"Enough of playing nursemaid to these overprivileged kids. They are violating curfew, we need to end this now. We should go in and grab them," said another cop.

Lights went on in the houses bordering Esther Beach Park.

It looked like a standoff to Edie. The girls weren't coming out of Lake Monona, and the cops weren't going in.

"What's the situation?" asked Edie.

One officer held out three bikinis.

Edie grabbed them. "Fucking damn. When does school start?"

"After Labor Day," said an officer.

"That late!" Edie turned toward the lake, floodlights highlighted three girls crouched down with their heads above water. "Hi girls, I'm Detective Swift. Who am I talking to?"

The girls' whispers carried over the water. "You talk, Barbie. This was your idea."

"Barbie," one girl called out.

"Well, Barbie, you and your friends are out

after curfew," said Edie from the water's edge. "Girls, do you understand how serious this is?"

No reply from the girls.

Edie tried again to get a conversation going between her and the girls. "How did you get out of the house without your parents' knowledge?"

The girls started whispering to each other. "Barbie, this is getting worse. We need to go home. You have to get us out of here." Every word was heard on shore.

Edie cut their secret negotiations short; she needed them to talk to her, not each other. "Girls, I'm wondering why you three decided to go skinny-dipping tonight?"

Dead silence.

Edie tried again. "Why did you three decide to go skinny-dipping tonight?"

"We were hot and tired of being locked in the house. And we didn't think anyone would be here," said Barbie.

"No one is, except three apparently naked girls and us eight cops. But someone did see you out past curfew and that someone called 9-1-1. Now here we all are; us on the beach and you naked in the lake. How are we going to solve this problem?"

"Who's the busybody?" Barbie shouted.

"Don't know," Edie replied.

"You guys go away and then we'll come out," yelled Barbie.

"We can't do that," Edie yelled back. She walked back to Deputy Garth Smith, dropped the bikinis next to him. "It doesn't look like they are coming out. I'm going in." She took off her shoes, socks, undid her duty belt, and handed it to Smith. "You are in charge of these. Garth, you have my back, right?" Edie didn't wait for confirmation before she dropped her slacks.

"Bikinis! Damn," said Smith. "I was in the office pool for you wearing thongs."

"Damn, I was certain she went commando," said Deputy Nordahl.

Edie knotted her service shirt under her breasts. She took her pistol back from Smith, dropped the magazine from the gun, and stuffed it into her bra. Edie made sure the gun was empty before flipping on the safety. Then she concentrated on the officers knotted around her. "Smith, I put my bet on you wearing tidy-whities. How about dropping your pants? I want to see if I win. And you, Nordahl, I don't see any pantie lines on you tonight, guess I was right when I put my money on you going commando. Why don't you both show us? I want to see if I win. Or are you too chicken? Baaaawwwk, baaaawwwk, baaaawwwk."

There were no takers.

Edie picked up the bikinis and walked into the lake. "Girls, I'm coming in. I've got your suits. One of you needs to meet me halfway."

"This is all your fault, Barbie. You go get them," said one of the girls.

The radio crackled on. "Report of shots fired in the vicinity of South Park Street."

"Get those girls out of the lake, we gotta go," yelled one of the Madison cops.

"Two of you go, the rest of us can handle this," Smith proposed to the Madison cop.

"What was that?" cried one of the lake girls.

Edie heard anxiety in the girl's voice. "Report of gunfire somewhere in Madison." Maybe that would push the girls out of the lake.

"I want to go home," was the collective cry from the girls. One of them started bawling.

Another one wailed, "I want my mama."

"Okay, okay, what I do for you bitches. Okay, I'll come and get them. But I want to see them in your hand," shouted Barbie.

Edie held the bikinis out at arm's length.

With a lot of splashing and squealing, Barbie popped out of the water, dashed to Edie, grabbed the suits, then plunged back into the lake.

Edie stood in the lake waiting for the girls while they wiggled into their suits, then followed them to shore. "You should've gone in, Smith, the lake was refreshing."

"My skinny-dipping days are over," said Smith. "I'm not letting anyone see my underwear except my wife and the guys at the gym, and they better not be looking at them too closely."

Edie dressed while the other officers took down names, addresses, and a short statement.

Nordahl escorted one of the girls to his squad. Edie restrained him, leaned in, and whispered, "No bouncing boobs in any of your reports. Understand?"

"You're taking the fun out of writing those things," he said.

"No boobs," Edie repeated.

Edie and Smith escorted the other two girls home.

"Is there an outbreak of stupid tonight?" asked Smith after they made sure each girl was in the custody of their parents.

"Probably. More likely a combination of groupthink with those girls and their brains seeing the challenge, not the consequences, of breaking the curfew—you know studies are showing they haven't reached their adult brains at that age," said Edie.

"You just sounded like Gracie," said Smith.

"Sorry, comes from hanging around her," Edie replied. "Pretty soon, I may sound like my toddler daughter."

"Oh God, what am I getting myself into having a kid?" said Smith.

"Smiles on your parents' faces. That kid will be your parents' revenge. They're probably praying right now that the kid will be just like you."

"They wouldn't do that, would they?"

"Every grandparent I talk to says it's enjoyable watching their kids parenting the next generation. They tell me it's a pleasure watching their own kids get a comeuppance."

"The what?"

"A comeuppance, a payback. I think that's why grandparents and their grandkids are so tight. Both like watching that middle generation squirm."

"I need to talk to Johnson, we need to get our stories straight," said Smith.

"Won't make a difference, your parents will snitch on you."

They stopped talking to listen to another dispatch—report of objects being thrown from the Lunde Lane overpass.

"Western Dane County," Edie and Smith said in unison.

"Seems as if stupid is pouring down on us tonight," said Edie. "Where to next, partner?"

"A dip in the lake?"

"Been there, done that. Back to the streets," said Edie.

It was one a.m. when Edie and Smith rendez-voused with Lieutenant Gracie Davis off Monona Drive.

Gracie handed cups to Edie and Smith, then

poured coffee from one of the many thermoses she had in her car. "Never pictured myself playing hostess for a bunch of cops by pouring coffee for them. Sorry, I forgot the tea cakes," she said.

"And cream and sugar," Edie added.

"The coffee is much appreciated," said Smith.

"Getting the stupid under control?" asked Edie.

"We get it under control in one area, and then it pops up in another. It's like playing whack-a-mole," said Gracie. "How's your night been?"

"One cranky reporter and three skinny-dipping girls," said Edie.

"I'm hoping for a January blizzard to blow through right about now," said Smith. "It would give something for people to complain about instead of sniping at each other."

"That's a great idea. Grumbling about the weather seems to be common ground for people around here. Maybe they'd be willing to stay off the streets then. Who was the reporter?" asked Gracie.

"Leigh Stone," replied Edie.

"Hope it wasn't too rough for you, Edie. She's never recovered from your first encounter," said Gracie.

"I handled it," said Smith.

"He did a fine job, too," said Edie.

"Hear she's moving to a bigger market, Miami possibly," said Gracie.

"How'd she score that?" asked Edie.

"A few of her stories are making some influential people squirm, a lot. Maybe the higher-ups in her business noted her effectiveness and paved the way for her move. Or someone wanted her out of their hair. Wonder where she's getting those stories?" said Gracie

"Reports of gunfire heard in the East Towne complex," the dispatcher reported.

Gracie capped the thermos. "The stupid rises again. See you there."

Edie and Smith dumped their coffee on the pavement and scrambled into their squad. By the time they got to the East Towne complex, the interstate ramps and the roads going into the complex had already been blocked off. Interstate 90/94 was backed up for miles in either direction. Edie and Smith were waved through the police stops and then assigned to assist with road closing at Lien and Thompson Road.

"Shit, I want to get in on the action, not patrol a roundabout," said Smith.

"We are in on the action. We're securing the area at Lien and Thompson. That could be where the gunfire came from. And be careful what you wish for, Smith. Think how happy this assignment will make your wife; a quiet area may help you make it to the birth of your baby."

"I hate roundabouts, now I'm stuck patrolling one."

"I haven't gotten used to them yet either. Don't think I'll need much coffee tonight. This adrenaline kick is going to keep me going for a while," said Edie.

"I need some antacids," said Smith.

"Nothing open for a few more hours," said Edie.

"Damn."

"Maybe it will all be over tomorrow."

"When the stores open, I'm stocking up on those antacids, just in case," said Smith.

Edie and Smith positioned their squad in the middle of Lien Road, and sat.

"Edie...?" Smith broke the silence,

"What do you want, Smith?"

"I'm curious, how long have you been on the force?"

"About ten years. Why?"

"Been telling my wife about our talks," said Smith. "You know she's a pretty good judge of character."

There was a pause.

"And?"

"What do you mean 'and'?"

"After a statement like that there's always a piece of advice tacked on," said Edie.

"Not advice, more of an observation. She was just wondering why you were talking so much about marriage. She thought you might be thinking about leaving the force. Maybe you have the ten-year itch and marriage would be a good excuse to leave."

"I'm not leaving the force. That doesn't mean I don't think about it, especially these days."

"I know."

"I didn't sign onto this job to be thanked, but I'd appreciate not being shot at," said Edie. "What about you? You thinking of jumping ship?"

"No. Not yet. The job is mostly interesting, punctuated with moments of terror with stretches of boredom. Like right now, I'd like to be moving the action along."

"Careful what you wish for," said Edie, opening her door. "I'm going to stretch my legs for a bit; otherwise, I'm going to snooze through the rest of this shift."

"Don't take forever, I need to get out of this car, too. I feel my butt spreading with all this sitting."

Edie did a few runners' stretches and then walked the road, keeping the car within a short running distance. The trees along the outer ring of the roundabout did nothing to hide all the stores on one side and all the apartments on the other. Probably a wetland the developers were required to keep. She'd never get used to endless apartment buildings; they might be a necessity of a town, but not the part of Madison she liked. She walked back to the squad and leaned against its trunk. Smith joined her.

"Another endless night," said Smith.

"That's pure poetry," replied Edie.

"Must be a residual effect of the English classes I had to take in college, don't go blabbing it around."

Edie stood up. "See that? There, on the other side of the roundabout?"

"Person out walking. Let's go see what they're doing out."

Edie and Smith got back in the squad. Edie called in the report.

Smith circled the roundabout counterclockwise, stopping the squad approximately twenty feet in front of the person. "What do you think? Male or female?"

"Can't tell, clothes are loose, long sleeves, long pants, long hair—nothing to make that determination. Sunglasses on," observed Edie.

"Addict?"

"Probably, or a really bad sunburn. But I'd go with probable addict. Let's find out." Edie opened her door and stood behind it. "Police, mind if we ask you a few questions?"

The person kept walking toward them.

Smith got out of the squad, keeping low. With the car between him and the walker, he positioned himself at the rear of the car.

"I need you to stop right now," Edie commanded.

The person stopped, looked around, and continued walking.

"I don't see any possible weapon. Do you, Smith?"

"Nope."

"I'm going to approach."

"I've got your back." He moved with the walker, stopping to shelter behind his car door.

Edie joined the person, keeping an arm's length-plus between them, and walked with him awhile. By that time she'd made her first assessment: definitely male, arms dangling at his side, skinny, but not an athletic skinny—sick skinny, sores on his face. "Evening, sir." Edie started the monologue. "This heat and curfew don't go together very well. Better if this happened during the winter. Which apartment do you live in? Do you have air-conditioning? This curfew would be a real bear to live through if you didn't. Hey, this looks like a good place to stop for a rest." They were standing in front of the squad. Her second assessment was the same. "Sir, would you please take off your sunglasses?"

After repeating the request a few more times, the man complied.

Wow, thought Edie, pinprick pupils at night. How did any light get into his brain? How was he able to function? "Sir, what is your name?"

"Excuse me, did you say something?" At least that is what he seemed to mumble.

"Can you tell me your name?"

"Fr...no, that's not it. It was just on the tip of my tongue. Give me a moment. What's your name?"

"Detective Swift."

"What do you do?"

"I look for stuff. I'm a detective with the sheriff's office."

Edie's peripheral vision caught Smith trying to control a laugh.

"Could you look for my name?"

"I need more information before I can do that."

"Okay, I'll wait for you to get it." The man slipped to the ground. Edie caught him before his head hit the pavement and gently lowered him down. "Smith, get me the naloxone. Then call for an ambulance."

Edie and Smith cleaned the area as the ambulance pulled away.

"Smith, this is all your fault, you wanted some action. Look what we got."

"This isn't the type of action I was looking for."

"Next time, be more specific."

Chapter 12

†

The last thing Edie remembered was putting a pillow over her face to block the sunshine. From what her watch was reading, it gave her two more hours of sleep. At that point, her body refused to sleep. She sat on the edge of her bed, holding her head in her hands. She knew she was at Aunt Jill's. But she didn't remember how she got there. Edie was naked; she surmised that she took off her clothes somewhere between the door and the bedroom. She was alone, she hoped. There was only one way to find out. She'd have to get out of bed. She pushed herself up, resisted the urge to flop back into to bed, took a deep breath, and went in search of her clothes.

They were on the kitchen floor. They stank. She carried them to the basement for washing. The place was cool. Maybe she should spend the rest of the day down there. Not a chance in hell of that happening, she told herself. If the curfew wasn't lifted, she'd be back on the streets working. She stuffed the clothes in the machine and went back upstairs.

Her brain fog hadn't lifted and she couldn't decide what to do next—heat water for coffee, or take a bath or maybe a shower. Or was it better to do it the other way around? She rested her head on the table as she thought the problem through.

Okay, first things first. She talked her way through filling the teapot with water, setting it on a burner, turning on the burner, then walking to the bathroom for a shower.

She turned on the water, stepped in, and jumped back out of the shower. Damn, it was cold. How did she forget how limited the supply of hot water was in this old house? There could only be one demand for hot water at a time. At least she was awake. She tested the water before getting back in. The lukewarm water did nothing to relax her muscles. The tension was still there, but the stench was gone. The teapot whistled. Another damn thing that needed her attention.

Cocooned in a blanket, a towel wrapped around her head, she sat sipping tea staring at the backyard. She began to relax, nothing demanding action from her. No diapers to change, no crying to soothe, no crazies out on the street, nothing that she had to do until the washing machine was done. Her phone ringing jolted Edie out of her reverie, she went in search of the noise. She found it in the bathroom. The missed call was from Phil. She called back.

"Sorry I missed the call. I'm enjoying a cup of tea right now; it's a pleasure sipping instead of gulping hot beverages. What's going on with you?"

"We were waiting for a call from you."

"Said I was sorry. I forgot how rough a twelve-hour shift is, and I might have a third one tonight. Took a few moments for myself, needed a breather from the world."

"You're a parent, you don't get any breathing time."

"How's Hillary?"

"She's crying for you."

"Hold the phone up to her ear, I'll talk to her."

"If I can catch her."

"What do you mean?"

"She's walking...remember?"

"I forgot, so sue me. Did you take some movies of her walking?"

"Yeah, I keep my smartphone with me."

"Send me all of the pictures."

"Don't know if I can get it all on one download. I know, come home and watch it firsthand."

"I'll be home tomorrow, no matter what happens with the curfew."

"Hillary will probably walk right past you, I've been teaching her not to talk to strangers."

"Are you getting a break? Who's helping you?"

"That's the other thing. Sage didn't make it home last night. Lisa wants you to look for her."

"Shit. I can't help right now. Has she filed a missing person's report? Tell me the whole story." Edie was now wide awake.

"From what Lisa says, Sage left here yesterday and never reached home."

"Matilda with her?"

"Matilda's at home."

"They need to report Sage missing ASAP. Did they give a good description of her? Do they have a current picture? Make of her car? Color? License plate number?"

"Already done. Walked Lisa through all that when she came looking for you to ask what she should do."

"Good thing you live with a cop."

"I don't want to be one, but it's okay if I'm married to one."

"We're not married."

"Why don't you come home and we can remedy that situation?"

"Sorry, I'm here until my next shift is done or this Madison thing blows over."

"Gotta go, Edie. Hillary's headed into the

bathroom. Call you later. Miss you. Love you. Marry me."

The connection was cut before Edie could answer. Her day was ruined and it hadn't even started.

Chapter 13

†

Edie was bouncing off the wall waiting for her clothes to dry. She went through all of the what-ifs surrounding Sage's disappearance. Crossed each one off and began again. Nothing was making sense. Aunt Jill's old house was too small to contain Edie and her exploding emotions.

She stepped outside of the house; it looked to her as if people were behaving normally in her old neighborhood. The kids were running through sprinklers; people were walking their dogs; others were in their cars heading to wherever. Then all the activity stopped, everyone seemed to be looking at her. Edie looked down. She was in her deputy uniform, she'd forgotten. All of those people seemed to be waiting for her to do something, so she did. She got in her car and waved to everyone as she drove out of what used to be her neighborhood—the house had been too small, the neighbors expected too much of her, she needed to be elsewhere.

From University Avenue, Edie took a left onto Walnut Street, which cut across the far end of the UW campus onto University Bay Drive. Her luck was changing. Lot 129 was empty. Normally it would be full of people using it as a staging area for a hike through Picnic Point—the students must not be back in town yet, and no one else had time for a frivolous mile and a half walk with the curfew coming in a few hours.

Edie sat on the hood of her car, her head resting in her hands, staring at the willows, the marsh beyond them, and the open waters of University Bay—a piece of nature in an increasingly noisy city that was calming Edie's soul.

The quiet didn't last. A car drove into the lot and parked next to her. She heard the car door open and then slam shut. "This place is empty. Why choose to park next to me? Go park far, far away, like over there in Lot 130," she yelled to the driver without looking around to see who it was.

"Didn't know you owned this place. I stopped because I was curious about the newest Thinker Statue on campus—was it real? A performance piece by a theater student? Or the newest creation by an art student? Could be a great story, I thought, and I drive in and find it is you. Then I remembered that Detective Edie Swift won't give me a story. I might be wasting my time here, I thought. But what the hell, I'll give it a try. What you staring at?"

Edie didn't need to turn around, the voice was familiar. "That bunch of willow trees. Leave me alone, Uselman. I got nothing for you."

"I've heard that before. I think you got a story, spill it. You owe me one."

"Not on your life. And I don't owe you nothing."

"Hey, we're buddies. We've been through murders, shootings, carjackings, student street parties gone crazy, and I haven't done you wrong."

"Yet. Are you following me?" Edie went back to looking at the willows and University Bay.

"No."

"Then why are you here?"

"Knew you'd be here. When you lived in Madison, this is where you'd come to think."

"You remember that?"

"Course I do. I keep track of my friends. Support them when needed."

Edie turned her gaze to Uselman; she needed to talk and Mark was the nearest living, breathing human; besides that, he knew stuff. She wouldn't have to fill him in on every little detail. "Okay. This is off the record."

It took Uselman a moment to reluctantly agree.

"Again, this is off the record. It's a personal story, not one of those how do women cops cope with family and a stressful job stories."

"Then I don't want to hear it. Go confess your sins to someone else. I don't like entanglements," said Uselman.

"Is that why you are not married?"

"One of them."

"What are the others?"

"I can't let go of the possibilities."

"What does that mean?"

"When I've stood up for friends at their weddings, I've noticed that each and every wedding vow included the bride and groom making a pledge to each other that they would forsake all others. When the lovebird made those vows, I'd look around the room and it always seemed to be overflowing with luscious women. Did those vows really mean that I was supposed to forsake each and every one of those lovely creatures? Why lie, I couldn't and still can't make that vow. The possibilities those women offered were enormous. Why stick with one when I could have many? How could I deprive myself of all the bounty this life has to offer? Maybe if I never needed to make that pledge, I could get married. But there that vow was, in each and every ceremony. Decided a long time ago that marriage wasn't for me."

A belly laugh erupted from Edie. She slid off her car and onto the ground to prevent a fall.

"Glad I amuse you," said Uselman. "Now tell me your story."

"It is still off the record," said Edie as she tried to control her laughter. "It's personal; one of the girls who babysits for me is missing."

"Ah, I can see my story, if you let me write it. It would be that something has penetrated your hard shell. I can see the lead: The softening of a hard-nosed cop."

"You don't have a story, remember?"

"What caused the crack?"

For a moment, Edie was silent. She'd met Uselman when she was a rookie cop, and was wary of him from the get-go. She'd learned quickly to set parameters to their friendship. After that happened, they became drinking buddies, and enjoyed each other's offbeat take on humanity, but their talks rarely delved into the deep personal stuff.

"It started with Phil, then the baby, then Troutbeck."

"So Phil was the snag that let the rest of the world flood in."

"More like trickle in. My baby opened the floodgates."

"My condolences, best of luck trying to save the world."

"What?"

"From what I've seen, every cop has the saving the world syndrome. You seem to have gotten an extra dose of it. How long have you been on the force?"

"About ten years."

"The cops have been my beat for a long time; most cops I know rethink their career after ten years on the job."

"Want to take a walk with me?"

"Thanks, but I've got to find someone I can quote. You going to be okay?"

"Sure, as soon as I can patch the hole in my armor." Edie returned to her perch on the hood of her car and went back to contemplating the willows along University Bay, and then Leigh Stone popped into her brain. Edie jumped off her car and reached Uselman before he got into his car.

"Reconsidering, Edie?" Uselman asked, hopefully.

"No. Wondering what you know about Leigh Stone."

"Not much. Why? Got a story about her?"

"Not really, met her on the street after curfew the other night. Heard she was moving to Miami. Thought you might know about how that happened."

"She's done some good in-depth stories recently. I'd love to know who her sources are, who greased her road to the top. By any chance, did you arrest her?"

"No. Cited her for curfew violation, then escorted her home."

"You should have arrested her, now that would have been a story." Uselman walked over to his car.

Uselman got in his car, waved at Edie as he drove away.

Edie didn't see, she was back to considering the willows off from Lot 129. She needed to get out of that place; it was attracting too many people. She looked over at Picnic Point; it was a nice walk, but usually a busy place. Hers was the only car in the lot, but you couldn't tell what the families of Eagle Heights were doing. Edie decided to chance it; at least she wouldn't be a sitting duck for everyone to stop and talk to her.

Picnic Point was all hers. The runners, hikers, and families that normally filled Picnic Point's paths were probably busy elsewhere. It was a pleasure to wander among the line of willows that started at Lot 129 and continued the all along the Point's shoreline. They framed the university buildings, and the Langdon Street frats and sororities, with the Capitol at the high point. It was lovely. Peaceful. A wonderful façade for the recent tragic deaths that now had her city in turmoil.

The Point had been one of her safe retreats as a student at UW-Madison, when books, papers, and regurgitating information on exams got to be too much. It felt like you were going to the end of the world. Mostly those student days were wonderful, but there were times when she needed to get away from it all. And a run to the end of Picnic Point fit the bill. Back then, she'd find a tree to sit in and let her legs dangle in Lake Mendota while she planned her future. Then a jog back to the main campus and everything seemed right again. Pleasant memories, but the past was no place to live.

At the tip of Picnic Point barriers and benches had been put up. To contain what? Natural erosion due to lake action? Stop people from walking out to the Point? They weren't effective. She walked around them and down to the water's edge and guessed that anyone who made it that far did also. Between her and Governor's Island on the far shore were miles of open water. It was inviting. "Fuck the present," she said, stripped off her clothes, hung them on the willow that skimmed the surface of the lake, and walked into the water.

A couple of front strokes took her away from land. She turned on her back and floated so she could watch the birds as they climbed, pivoted, and dove between her and the universe. Enthralled by the silence of the place, Edie was unaware of how far she had drifted until she turned her head and saw the homes of Shorewood Hills. The village wasn't around the bend anymore; it was in plain sight. She flipped onto her belly and tread water. Governor's Island seemed a lot closer. Edie continued to tread water as she identified Madison's landmarks. The skyline views of her city didn't do it justice. The walk and swim brought back pleasant memories but there was only one way to go—forward. She swam back to shore.

Edie sat naked on a stone bench drying in the sun and staring at the wall holding a quote by Aaron Bohrod, a past artist-in-residence at the university, about getting inspiration from nature. She considered the incongruity of the wall between her and nature. The birds, the woods, and a few sailboats on the other side of the lake kept her company. The tension slipped away, her shoulders relaxed. In a better world, she would have sat there for hours, but the sun moved lower in the sky, the shadows lengthened. Edie put on her clothes; it was time for her to go back to work.

Chapter 14

†

"**W**hat the hell is the matter with you, Edie?" Smith yelled.

Edie, sitting next to him, yelled back. "Find a quiet street and pull over."

"Which one? They're all quiet."

"Then pull over here."

Instead, Smith pulled into the nearest parking lot off of Monona Drive.

For Edie, sitting in the squad brought back the feeling of uselessness that the swim had washed away. She needed action. Edie got out of the car, slammed the door shut, and stomped up and down the empty parking lot. It didn't help. There was no way to escape the helplessness she was feeling. As a cop she swore to protect and serve. Duty called, she came and was doing her job while her family and friends, half a county away, needed her as much. And she could do nothing for them. She continued to stomp up and down the parking lot. The stomping didn't ease the tension and it didn't solve her dilemma.

Smith got out of the car, leaned against it, positioned himself to stand watch over Edie and the road.

A Dane County squad car pulled in next to Smith. Gracie rolled down the window. "What's happening?"

"Edie's got a stick up her ass. And I'm making sure nothing harms her...and vice versa."

"Need a break?"

"Yeah, and a cold beer."

"Out of luck on that last one, Smith, but I'll relieve you for a bit," said Gracie. She dug into her pocket and pulled out a wad of bills. "There's a coffee shop across the road that's still open. Buy each of us a cup of coffee and whatever else they have to munch on. I'll stand watch over Edie."

Smith walked over to the shop. Gracie took Smith's post and watched Edie stomp up and down the parking lot.

At least I'm doing something, thought Edie, oblivious to the change of the guard watching over her.

"What the fuck's the matter with you, Detective Edith Swift?" Gracie yelled.

That voice brought back Edie to the here

and now. Gracie was one of the few people who ever called her Edith. She turned and yelled back, "Troutbeck has me by the throat and I'm stuck here."

"I understood none of that. Quit that tantrum, it's unbecoming to an officer of the law and come over here and say it again to me, in a civilized tone."

Edie gave up the stomping and walked over to Gracie, then leaned against the squad next to her. "One of my babysitters is missing and I can't do anything about it."

"If it's been reported, then one or more of our deputies will be looking for her. Your assignment is here. You have to trust your fellow officers to do their jobs. And you have to do the job that's in front of you. Stay focused, Edie. Maybe when this crisis is over you can look for her. But this crisis ain't over. I need you in the here and now. Don't get distracted, that's when we get hurt or do something stupid."

"I'm trying to stay focused here. But sitting in a car driving up and down these streets isn't easy. I want to yell at everyone to grow up, but I don't. I keep a lid on my own thoughts and actions, but at the same time, I also need to be looking for Sage. But I can't because I swore that I would help keep Madison quiet. But all I'm doing is sitting in a car. Damn it, I've got too many buts to consider. Double damn it. I've got a gut feeling about that girl. I don't like what I've seen of her family dynamics."

"Tell it to whoever got the assignment to look

for her. For now, back off from that case. Your job is here. Now."

"Not that easy to back away when it involves Troutbeck."

"What! They think you walk on water?"

"And that I can outthink Sherlock Holmes."

"When did you start doing that? They haven't known you too long, have they?" asked Gracie.

"Long enough to make me a superhero."

"Time will change that attitude. Don't let their adoration go to your head. You know you can't do any of that stuff."

Edie and Gracie each folded their arms over their chests, leaned against the squad, and stared across the empty parking lot.

"How's this thing going to end?" asked Edie.

"This time, I hope with a whimper, but at some point the uneasiness under the surface in this country may explode in this city. We can't escape it forever. Culture clashes are happening across our country. They will come here too. Whether we want them to or not."

"What is this country thinking? The law be damned? Equal opportunity be damned? Everything be damned? Forget about everyone else in this country and grab what you can for yourself? Selfishness rules? Forget that Americans were going to forge a new person from people seeking a new beginning, a new world? Forget that we're in this together? When did we stop believing in each other? When did we stop believing in a better future?"

"Didn't know you were a true believer of the American idea. Right now it seems as if this equality jargon was just a bone to placate us. For the black people I know, it's been hard to erase the collective memories of the abuse we took, the damages it did to our souls. Maybe the stench of slavery could have been washed away if slavery had been allowed to die. But it morphed into Jim Crow. We've been climbing out of that hole for decades now; it sure seems as if some people want to kick us back into that hole." Gracie stopped for a moment, then added, "But... but I can't say the law and society hasn't helped me. Look where I am now. Me—a black woman—is a lieutenant in the Dane County Sheriff's Office. Think of that! Me, coming from nothing and rising to this level."

"Me, too. If those opportunities hadn't opened up, I'd probably be sitting behind a desk typing away, bored out of my skull and being someone's little woman."

"No, I think you'd be out blocking traffic and smashing windows to get society's attention about the wrongs of the world. Glad you're still on this side of the law. I know that if I weren't wearing this uniform, I would be fighting at the barricades.

Some days I wonder why I don't quit and start leading the charge toward change myself."

"I thought I could make more significant changes from the inside," said Edie.

"Ah, our youthful idealism. Don't know if we were stupid or arrogant back in those days. So... we'll do our smashing from the inside, help get things changed. What do you say, Edie? Care to keep going?"

"I prefer to think of it as instituting changes for the benefit of all."

"I'll take that, sounds noble. Those changes have been a long time in coming, wish they'd come a little faster."

"I hear you. Changes aren't moving very fast outside of the department, either. I'd like it if, when I walked into a restaurant or bar, people would see more than my long legs and boobs. I've got a brain."

"What are you talking about, girl? You got your whiteness giving you some protection. I walk into a business and everyone is watching my every move, and probably counting their merchandise after I leave."

"Hell, I won't go into a bar alone. Every guy in there thinks it's an invitation to hit on me."

"I hear you on that one. I go into a bar, even with Martin, and I can see men eyeing me up, trying to figure out if he's my pimp and what it will cost to have sex with me—money and a few drinks or will they have to use force. Why am I not a person? Why can't they see that I am a person? It is such a simple thing to do. Is that impossible to see me as a person?"

"Haven't made much progress, have we?" said Edie.

"I understand about that bar thing," Smith said, coming up behind them. He handed coffee to Gracie and Edie, and opened the box of bars and donuts. "These are on me, a closing special."

"What do you know about sexual harassment?" asked Edie.

"Maybe not as much as you two do, but I've experienced it. Let me tell you a story. But before I do, you gotta promise not to tell anyone. No one. Especially not Ben. Do you understand?" said Smith.

Edie and Gracie promised him their silence while giving the Girl Scout salute, which they had never been but they didn't inform Smith of that fact, and then crossed their hearts that they would never tell anyone—especially not Ben Harris.

Smith accepted their pledges. "Well, one day, right after a run, I stopped in at a local bar for a brewski—never been in that bar before. There I was standing at the counter drinking my beer, dripping sweat on my already drenched running shorts and T. Pretty soon I noticed some guy was standing next me. He started commenting on how sweaty and fit I looked. He kept inching toward me. I looked around the place, noticed there were only men in the place, and that they were all staring at me. I felt like a piece of meat. Didn't they see my wedding ring? Wasn't their gaydar or something working? Finished the brew and then hightailed it out of there—faster than a Favre's pass ever flew."

Edie spit out her coffee as she doubled over in laughter.

Gracie turned her back on Smith, but her coffee was gushing down the side of the cup from the increasing pressure of her hand.

"What, what's so funny? I wasn't going to waste a Spotted Cow."

"Report of objects being thrown from Haight Road overpass," squawked from the radio.

"How many does that make, Edie?" Smith asked.

"Two that I know of," Edie replied.

"Sounds like some adolescents with time on their hands. We need rain or school to start, better if both of those happened. You two okay here?" said Gracie.

"Yeah," said Edie.

"Sure," said Smith.

"Then I'm checking out that outbreak of stupid. Now get your butts off my car. And Smith, if this food is on you, you can leave my money on my desk."

For Edie and Smith, it would be another long night of maintaining quiet in the streets of Madison and the highways leading into it.

Chapter 15

†

Through bloodshot eyes, Edie saw the sun rise in a red sky. "Smith, you ever hear that old saying about skies?" she asked, taking the cup of coffee Smith offered her.

"Which one?"

Edie took a sip of cold coffee before continuing. "Red skies in the morning, sailors take warning. Red skies at night, sailors delight."

"Don't remember that one. What does that got to do with us? We're not at sea," said Smith.

"If it applies to us landlubbers, we're in for a storm," said Edie.

"That would be great. Please hurry it up; maybe a storm will cool everyone off, at least keep them inside longer. I'm tired of these streets."

"I'm starting to agree. I'm hoping that the September rains come early."

Edie and Smith leaned against their patrol car and searched the western horizon for signs of a storm.

"Don't see anything," said Smith.

"Can't you feel the breeze, smell the scent of rain?" asked Edie.

"Nope."

"When rain hits..." Edie broke off her explanation about petrichor and the release of aerosols and answered her phone. "Detective Swift..." followed by lots of ahhs, mmms, and a few yeses. She hung up, took a few sips of coffee, and dumped the rest on the ground.

"Well?" said Smith.

"We're relieved. We're supposed to go in, write up our reports, and then go home."

"I've been waiting for this for seventy-two hours." He dumped his coffee and quickly got into the squad. "Detective, get your ass in here, we are on a mission."

"Hold on for a moment, I'm savoring the coming storm."

"If it comes, I'd rather enjoy it snuggled next to my wife. Get in here."

The rain didn't hit until Edie was driving home. She rolled down her car window partway to catch the sweet scent of rain and let the rain wash away some of the heat and grime.

Hours later Edie woke to the sweet scent of rain and something warm snuggling in her arms. It was Hillary.

Edie glanced toward Phil, who was framed by the bedroom door and smiling. "Why isn't she in her own bed?"

"I'm not a heartless bastard. She's been crying for her mother for the last three days. Now here you are. If she wants to be next to you, she gets to be there. Her wish is my command."

"She could have..."

"Look around, see the pillows all around our baby, and the chairs pushed against the bed? And I checked on the two of you, often." Phil paused for a moment. "I'm kind of jealous of that little girl. She's in my place."

"Why not join us?"

Phil walked to the bed, knelt down by Edie. "Wanted to keep my women happy. You two looked so contented snuggling together, I didn't want to disturb that. And I want you to myself."

Edie put an arm around Phil's shoulder and pulled him in for a long kiss.

Phil broke the embrace. "More of that later. How'd it go?" he whispered.

"Last night was quiet. So far the violence has been contained. We kept outbreaks of anger and discontent to small areas. Only a few pockets of anger erupted. Full-blown socioeconomic war hasn't broken out, hope that never happens. Racial tensions in the city have burned themselves out... for now, but they are bubbling under the surface. We need to do work on fixing those problems."

"What, oh wise and wonderful Troutbeck hero, should we do?"

"Cut that out. Remember, you helped put me in that position. But my short answer is—live up to our American ideals."

"If anyone still believes in them anymore. What stopped the violence?"

"Don't know. Maybe us police being out in force, maybe the curfew, maybe the rain, maybe the anger petered out, maybe cooler heads prevailed. There are lots of maybes that I can't think of right now. The short of it is, I don't know. I can wait for the official report to come out. I am not looking forward to the next time there's an eruption. Madison can't escape trouble forever." Edie tried to reposition Hillary closer to the pillow barrier. Hillary moved, opened one eye, and stared at her mother. Edie stopped moving.

Phil giggled. "Serves you right for not coming home sooner. She needs to sleep some more; she didn't sleep very well when you were gone. So you are stuck here until she wakes up. I'll make supper."

"Good. I'm tired of canned soup and deli food."

"Canned soup! You were in Madison. Why didn't you eat out?"

"Only had my uniform and it stank after a night of patrolling and I didn't want to panic everyone by going into a business nude or in uniform. Have I mentioned how tired I was after patrolling all night?"

"Should have called me, I know the best restaurants that deliver."

Phil kissed Edie and stood up. "Glad you're home. I'll call you when supper is ready."

Edie spent the next hour staring at her daughter, then the ceiling, then the rain falling outside her window, and then back again at Hillary. Her arm was going to sleep. But she didn't want to chance getting the one-eyed evil stare of her daughter. Edie didn't budge an inch.

Chapter 16

†

Hillary became Edie's shadow. Where Edie went, Hillary followed. Hillary sat on the floor of the bathroom and watched as Edie took a shower and used the toilet. Hillary stood next to Edie as she dressed, blocked her exit when Edie wanted to step outside, and insisted that she sit on Edie's lap and share her supper of Caprese salad, bratwurst parboiled in beer, and raspberries over New York vanilla ice cream. Edie got to eat the tomatoes and basil, while Hillary ate all the mozzarella, part of the brat, and more than her share of the dessert. "Garden fresh tomatoes. Never knew what I was missing when I was a kid. Where'd you get them from?"

Phil stared at his plate before replying. "My mother brought the tomatoes and raspberries."

"Nothing wrong with that. Why do you look so guilty?"

"My mother's reason for coming over. She wanted to know her granddaughter better, in case something happened to you."

Edie placed her fork on the plate. "That's nothing new for her. I've never been good enough for her darling boy. I suspect there's more that you aren't telling me. What the f— "

"Watch the language around Hillary. She's trying out lots of words these days."

"What the frick did she do this time?"

"Better you don't know, and better I don't say. I didn't take the bait."

Edie took a deep breath in and let it out slowly, several times. "First she hounded me, and you, about us not being married. What is it this time?"

"Hillary's the last of the line with the Best name. She'd like me to have another kid."

"Seriously?"

"Yes."

"Has she chosen the other woman?"

Phil kept his eyes glued on the last of the raspberries and ice cream.

"She has chosen one. What the hell! Does she ever bother your sisters like that? Why doesn't your mother bribe one of your sisters into changing their kids' last name?"

"They changed their names when they got married. Now they're only half Bests."

"So are you and so is your daughter. And your

mother is only a Best by marriage. Has she ever thought of that?"

"She hasn't been able to grasp that concept. She wants a grandson from me to carry on the name."

"And you? What do you want?"

"I'm not going to oblige her. Hillary is a bonus, but the person I want in my life is you. Marry me."

"Why change the arrangement?"

"Sex."

"Duh. Not getting enough? Any more convincing arguments?"

"Public commitment."

"I should have you committed."

"Edie, you know what I mean."

"What else do you have?"

"Companionship."

"I'm here, you're here, we're all here."

"This conversation seems to always come back at me. Why?" Phil observed.

"You are doing the asking. Can we change the subject?"

"Sure. Aunt Jill wants to talk to you."

"About what?"

"She didn't say."

"Do you have any idea what it's about?"

"Nope."

"A moment ago, you were full of questions and answers. Surely you asked Aunt Jill what it was she wanted?"

"She wouldn't say."

"Can you watch Hillary while I go talk with Aunt Jill?"

"Nope, your turn to watch her."

"After I put her to bed, can you watch her?"

"Yes. What are you going to do?"

"Get my haircut."

"Doesn't look like you need it."

"That's because I get it cut on a regular schedule, and I am now overdue for a cut. Why are you so testy?"

"I've been holding down the fort recently. I need some time for myself and my business. And I need Hillary's sleeping time to be our time. Our daughter wasn't the only one missing you. When do I get some time? After Aunt Jill? After Sage?"

"Later. Damn, I forgot about Sage."

"I didn't, if Lisa isn't calling, she's knocking on our door looking for you."

"Okay. My new plan is I put Hillary to bed, then I go to Carole's, after that, it's you and me. Are you okay with that?"

"You'll run like the wind through Troutbeck so no one can see you? You won't let anyone stop you?"

"It's raining. I'll take the car."

"Deal."

The baby was asleep. Troutbeckians were

settling in for the night. And as she drove through the town Edie tried to keep her eyes on the road as she drove to Carole's; she didn't want to make eye contact with anyone. But she couldn't keep her eyes focused on the straight and narrow. She had to see what was happening in Troutbeck. The VandenHuevel house was dark except for the front room, where light was peeking through at the edges of the curtains. The sold sign unbelievably still hung in front of the corner store. A deputy's squad was parked at the side of the church waiting for speeders. Edie crept through the rest of Troutbeck. At Carole's she ran from the car to the salon, and then flopped into a chair for more than a haircut.

Carole was waiting for her. "Driving your car isn't fooling anyone. We all know what kind of car you drive, and we all know you're home. Has Lisa been to see you yet?"

"No. I'm hoping to sleep in tomorrow before I'm bombarded with the problems of Troutbeck."

"Just a haircut tonight?"

"I want the works."

"Bring any money? Sage's cut took some time. She also added a generous tip to the bill."

"At your suggestion? Hell, I can afford it; I've put in a lot of overtime recently."

"Glad to see some of that public money circulating my way. Haven't heard from you for a few days. I was beginning to wonder if you might have skipped town to avoid paying your bill."

"Leave you? Never. You're my source for all that's going on in this burg. Anything new?"

Carole eased the chair to a semi-reclining position and then ran the warm water through Edie's hair. "Didn't Phil pass on the news?"

"No."

"Corner store's been sold, haven't heard who bought it. Harold's got grumpier since Sage disappeared, keeps coming over here asking about you. Lisa stops in too. Didn't have the heart to tell them I'm not your keeper. Looks like you've become the local miracle worker."

"No, I'm not. I am just doing my job, which is to keep on a case until it's done or the leads have gone cold. Carole, I don't think I can take this case."

"Why not?"

"As I've been telling everyone, I'm too close to the people involved. The expectations from this community about my abilities are over the top. What if I make assumptions and follow them instead of following the facts? What if I push other deputies on the case into thinking my way? What if I miss something?"

"What if you don't?"

"Believe me, this time it's better for me to be on the sidelines."

"You solved two murder cases that hung like a black cloud over this town."

"Anyone could have done it."

"They didn't, you did."

"Are you trying to push me into working on this case?"

"I'm trying to get you to talk to a neighbor who is desperately missing her niece. Think of what Matilda must be going through." Carole abruptly released the wash chair. Edie grabbed the arms of the chair to keep from flying out of it. Carole nodded for Edie to go to the cutting station.

"You sound angry. Can I comb out my own hair?"

"Do it at your own house, and then cut your own hair."

"Why the anger?"

"You brought a little bit of sanity back to this place. We need you again. Sage is missing, a girl I've known since before she was born, and you are refusing to help. Why not help this time? Why?"

"I don't always solve people's problems. I'm not always a cop."

"Like hell you're not," said Carole. She stopped forcing the comb through Edie's tangled hair, twirled the chair around so she and Edie were face to face, and began waving the comb at Edie. "In this town, I'm always the hairdresser, the historian is always the historian, Bridget will always be a high school principal, and Harold will always be the guy who sticks his nose where it doesn't belong."

"Okay, I'll talk to Lisa. And I'll come back another day for a trim when you've calmed down."

"When will you talk to Lisa?" Carole demanded, still pointing the offending hair comb at Edie.

"Tomorrow," said Edie, taking the comb from Carole. "Hand over that comb, it's become a dangerous weapon in your hand. My head can't take any more of your combing."

"Fair enough." She let the comb go without a struggle. "What's new at home?"

"Hillary's walking."

"Sera gave me the details and showed me the video."

"See, you know everything that happens in this burg. Maybe you should be tracking down Sage."

Chapter 17

†

Edie answered the front door while sipping her first cup of coffee. "Luke, what brings you out here?"

"Morning, Edie." Detective Luke Fitzgerald's face turned a bright red. He looked down at the step. "Am I interrupting something?"

Edie followed his gaze down, her bathrobe was mostly open. "Luke, after all you've seen as a detective, you can blush at this? Here, hold this." She handed her cup to Luke, rearranged the robe and tightened the belt. "Better?"

"Yeah." He looked up, but the blushing continued.

She took back the cup. "Want something to eat?"

"Thanks, but I really just came to see Phil. Is he in?"

"He's in the kitchen, giving Hillary her breakfast."

"Is he decent?"

"What do you mean?"

"Does he have clothes on?"

"Luke, grow up." Edie led the way to the kitchen and sat down to finish her breakfast.

"Hi, Luke, want some coffee?" Phil asked as he finished wiping up Hillary's spills.

"Sure."

"Pour yourself a cup. Cups are in the cupboard. Milk's in the fridge."

Luke went through the cupboards until he found a cup, filled it with coffee, and sat down at the table.

Phil rinsed out the rag and sat opposite Luke. Neither said a word.

Edie took the lead. "Luke, I'm assuming you didn't come all the way out here for a cup of coffee. Since you asked for Phil, who is sitting across from you in case you've forgotten what he looks like, I'm guessing you have some official police business with him. Why don't you start the conversation?"

"It's weird having you sit in on this," said Luke.

"Why? Never bothered you before. If you want, I can turn my back or sit somewhere else."

"But you'll be here, and you'll still be Edie Swift."

"No different from any other detective."

"Yes, you are."

"Luke, I'm not leaving. I don't know why you're

here, but since you came to see Phil, do what you have to do."

Luke turned to talk to Phil. "Okay with you, Phil?"

Phil nodded.

"Okay then, this is the second time one of your trucks has been hit by water balloons."

This was news to Edie. She tried to get Phil to look at her; even kicking him in the shins didn't get his attention.

Phil gave Luke his undivided attention. "Yes. Different trucks, different drivers."

"Why do you think this is happening?"

"I don't know, was hoping you could tell me."

"Know of anyone holding a grudge against you?"

"Nope. Don't have any disgruntled employees that I'm aware of, and I haven't fired anyone. My customers seem to be happy. The TV news reports suggest that this is probably kids with time on their hands."

"Could be. Your business was vandalized earlier this year, wasn't it?"

"Yes. Have you caught anyone yet?"

"Not yet. Have there been any other incidents at your shop? Any damage done to your trucks or building?"

"No damage to either, only a few pissed-off drivers and a few scared ones after those water balloons were thrown. A few of the drivers are talking about carrying guns on their runs."

Luke finished his coffee. Flipped his notebook shut. "That's not a good idea. If you think of anything else, call me, okay?"

"Yes, he will," said Edie, rising from her chair.

"Don't get up, Phil. I think I can find my way out," Luke said.

Phil was clearing the table before Luke left the kitchen.

Edie leaned against the sink, watching Phil avoid her gaze. When she heard the front door close and Luke's car start, she dumped her coffee in the sink. Her anger about Phil keeping her in the dark about his trucks being targeted exploded. "What the—"

"Excuse me, what did I tell you about your language?"

"Don't sidetrack this conversation. Hillary can impress her future classmates with her knowledge and correct usage of a certain part of our language. She'll be a hit on the playground."

"Don't start the lessons now. She'll say those words in front of my mother. I don't need another lecture from her."

"Don't change the subject, Phil. When I was on patrol, I'd heard reports about trucks being water-bombed, didn't know they were yours. When were you going to tell me that they were your trucks?"

"You were busy. You didn't need one more thing to worry about."

"I'm not the little woman. In my job, one more worry isn't going to matter. I'm being pushed into looking for Sage by all of Troutbeck and you, so why are you keeping me out of your problem?"

"I'm aware that we co-mingled our lives, but this isn't your case."

"But you are."

"Then we are going to make it official?"

"Stay focused here, Phil."

"Can't, someone's at the door."

Edie, still in her bathrobe, answered the door. "Johnson!"

"Morning, Edie."

"Come on in. My house seems to be the popular coffee stop for cops today. You just missed Luke Fitzgerald. See anybody else from the department on the road?" Edie stepped outside, and then looked up and down the road to ascertain the situation for herself.

"I'm the only one. What I really came to talk to you about is Sage Staley."

"Do it over a cup of coffee. Come on back to the kitchen. Phil, we got another one," she yelled back to him.

"Who is it this time?" Phil shouted.

"Johnson." Edie led the way to the kitchen, and then settled into her rocking chair.

"Well, deputy, this is a self-serve place. Cups are in the upper cupboard, looks like there is still coffee in the pot, and milk's in the fridge," said Phil, taking Hillary out of her high chair.

Johnson poured himself a mug.

Edie motioned Johnson into the chair opposite her rocking chair. "What do you need to know?"

Johnson set his mug on the cold wood stove, took out his notebook and pen, and sat down. "Am I keeping you from something, Edie?"

"Not really. My time is yours."

"What can you tell me about Sage Staley?"

"Sage and her cousin Matilda VandenHuevel sit for me on occasion. I believe they are the same age. Those two seem very close. The three of us were stargazing last Saturday. Last Friday, Phil and I ran into her and her family at the Sweet Corn Festival. That's about all I know."

"Why were you stargazing?"

"Matilda is an amateur astronomer; she was pointing out the shooting stars to us. She's a born teacher."

"How does Sage fit into what you've been telling me?"

"What I said before, she was up visiting her cousin, comes up to Troutbeck quite often. When

Sage is in Troutbeck, she tags along with Matilda when I need a sitter."

"Do you know what might have happened to Sage?"

"No clue. I was on patrol in the Madison area when it occurred. I haven't talked to anyone in town about Sage's disappearance. Have you talked to her father?"

"No, I've asked their local police to talk to her parents. What is your impression of Sage?"

"She's intelligent, determined. I hear from her aunt, Lisa VandenHuevel, that she's become rebellious, causing turmoil in her family."

"Is Sage a problem?"

"Not around me and not that I'm aware of."

"Anything else you can tell me?"

"I think I mentioned her father. I'm curious about the family dynamics."

"What do you know?"

"Nothing, just a gut feeling that not everything is kosher there. I'd like to learn more about that family dynamic."

"About who?"

"Everyone in Sage's immediate family. When I met them at the Sun Prairie Corn Fest, I kept getting a feeling that there's a disconnect between what I've been told and what I saw of that family, but I haven't figured out what it is yet. Sage is up here a lot, and what she says about her family is different from what Matilda and Lisa VandenHuevel say."

"Are you taking over this case?"

"I don't plan on it. Sage has sat for my kid. I don't want what I might find nor don't find be tainted by that association. Ren, you need to know that my neighbors are pushing me into investigating her disappearance."

"I thought that might happen. My neighbors do the same to me. I figure it's just part of the job. But I need to know that you'll keep me in the loop on this, if you find anything."

"I don't want to step on your toes, Ren, but if I look into the case, yes, I will keep you informed."

"Anything else you'd like to add, Edie?"

"No."

Johnson snapped his notebook shut. "Then I'll be going. Thanks for the coffee."

Edie walked him to the door. "Have you talked with the police in Sage's hometown?"

"Yeah. We're coordinating our efforts in finding the girl. Since she disappeared from here, we're taking the lead."

"Have they talked with her parents?"

"I assume so, but I'll check to see what they found," Johnson said as he stood at the door. "Edie, next time I'm here, could you be dressed?"

Edie looked down, her bathrobe was open.

"I've nothing to hide, Johnson, and you've seen my boobs before."

Johnson opened the door. Lisa VandenHuevel was on the other side. Edie readjusted her bathrobe and tightened and knotted the belt.

"Edie, sorry to interrupt you this way, but I saw a sheriff's car in your driveway. I was hoping that it would be Deputy Johnson. And it is. I am so happy to see you two working together on finding Sage. Is there something new? What can I tell my sister?"

"Sorry, ma'am, nothing new at this time. We're interviewing anyone who has had contact with Sage since she's been in Troutbeck," said Johnson.

"Oh, I thought there might be something... silly me, what was I thinking, Edie's just started on the case."

"Your concern is understandable, Mrs. Vanden-Huevel," Johnson said. "Detective Swift and I will be keeping each other informed of any developments concerning your niece's disappearance."

"This is wonderful, just wonderful; we now have the A-team working for Sage! That is something good I can tell Lindsey. Thank-you, thank-you, thank-you, Edie. And you too, Deputy Johnson." Lisa stepped off the step and practically skipped down the driveway. She waved at Aunt Jill, who was pulling into the drive.

"Busy place," Johnson observed.

"And I'm not even dressed," said Edie. "Looks

like I've been pushed into the case...unofficially, keep me updated. Okay?"

"Sure thing," said Johnson as he left.

"Holding court in your PJs?" Aunt Jill asked, stepping off the sidewalk to let Johnson pass.

"Can't, don't have any on. Are you watching Hillary here or at Hank's?"

"Both. We'll start out at Hank's, maybe we'll stay there, I don't know. Any word on Sage?"

"Et tu?"

"Edie, you've got to understand that this little burg thinks you have superpowers."

"Does that include you?"

"No. I knew you when your only superpower was trouble."

"If only Troutbeck knew my past."

"They wouldn't believe any of it. From the way Lisa was acting, looks as if she's conned you into taking on her problem. Think you could use some R&R from this place?"

"Yeah, and some from my life."

"How about a day off? Just you and me kiddo, we haven't done that since Hillary's birth. We could spend a day hiking the bluffs at Devil's Lake, then maybe hike up Gibraltar Rock."

"Don't have a day to spare."

"Can you find a few hours?"

"Maybe. Where you thinking of going?"

"Manna, Chocolatier, Lazy Jane's, Marigold, your choice."

"All good places, but I don't know when I'll have time to spare."

"You have to learn to make time, Edie. Set a date, the sooner, the better. Where's Hillary now?"

"I think Phil is getting her ready."

Squeals were coming from the hallway. Both women rushed toward the sound. Hillary was swaying from side to side as she walked down the hall with Phil close behind. Aunt Jill scooped up Hillary, mile-wide smiles spread across each of their faces.

"Looks like I'm outranked here, you two have a good day," said Edie, kissing her daughter and her aunt. She walked to the kitchen. Aunt Jill followed with Hillary.

"Edie?" Aunt Jill began.

"Yes?" Edie replied as she filled the dishwasher.

"Edie."

Edie turned to face her aunt. "What's wrong?"

"It isn't me. One of the girls at Hank's place seems to be having a problem. Says she's seen a car sitting across from the farm a few times, it's making her nervous."

"Anything happen?"

"No, I don't think so, at least nothing she'll tell me about."

"Has she reported it to the police?"

"Edie, you know the problem. How can an undocumented worker report anything to anyone in the government without being deported?"

"Shitty, isn't it? This idiotic xenophobia is hobbling us cops. We can't even help people who might need it because they're scared of what might happen. When did we become an asshole nation?"

"Don't ask me, my generation was supposed to make the world better, not worse. But I can help that young girl with her little problem—I have you to help."

"Okay, I'll put on my superhero costume for you. Does this girl remember anything about this car?"

"White, four doors with rust around the bottom of the door, only has a back license plate, license plate number starts with RBR, and the man is very thin with a hole in the front of his neck."

"Sounds like that girl has an excellent memory. We could use her in the department. I'll start looking into it. Until I can look into it, would you feel more comfortable staying here with Hillary than out at Hank's place?"

"No, I'm not scared, just concerned about that young girl. Hopeful now that you are looking into it. Want to come for supper?"

"We'll take you up on that, I'm tired of eating my own cooking," said Phil, walking into the kitchen. "Where will we be eating, in Madison or at Hank's?" He handed Aunt Jill the diaper bag.

"Hank's. No food left to speak of at my house."

"I know," said Edie.

"See you later," said Phil, kissing Hillary, Aunt Jill, and Edie goodbye. "That look is good around the house, but will it work out on the street?" he whispered to Edie.

"Never know, might stop criminals in their tracks."

"It does me, every time," said Phil.

Fifteen minutes later, Edie was dressed for work and sitting in her car at the corner stop sign waiting for the forage wagons and semitrucks hauling vegetables from the fields to pass—it was that time of year when the veggie trucks owned the road, and, if she remembered correctly, another month before the fall harvest was in full gear and she'd have to watch out for lots of slow-moving vehicles. On the other side of the road she saw Harold Acker was shuffling home from his morning visit to his wife's grave. He looked up, saw Edie, and waved her over.

When the last forage wagon had passed, she pulled the car next to him and rolled down the passenger-side window.

Harold leaned in. "You find that little girl," he

commanded, then stepped away from Edie's car and continued his slow walk home.

Edie banged her head against the steering wheel. When she sat up, she felt something warm and wet trickling down her face. A glance in the mirror confirmed it was blood. Putting pressure on the wound, she searched the car for a Band-Aid and, not finding one, she drove out to the highway with one hand pressed against her forehead.

Chapter 18

†

If it wasn't one thing, it was another. Three days' worth of e-mails to sort through, follow-up calls to make, and new cases to review made Edie late for dinner. Why couldn't crime take a holiday? Edie pulled into her driveway. Maybe all of us could arrange to meet on a beach somewhere sunny, relax, and not think about anything or act on it, just be.

After turning off the car, Edie sat and tried not to think, and then noticed that Phil and Sera were sitting on the front step talking. They were still talking when she kicked the car door open and slammed it shut. They still didn't acknowledge her. Edie walked over to the step and stood quietly in front of them.

Phil looked up. "Edie, when did you get home?"

"A few hours ago. What are you two talking about?"

"My father," said Phil. "What's that on your forehead?"

"A Band-Aid. I'm okay, thanks for asking."

"I'll be the judge of that," Phil said, standing up for a closer look at Edie's injury.

"I knew your dad in high school," said Sera, continuing the conversation with Phil. "Nice guy. You remind me of him, sweet and fun."

Phil carefully loosened the edge of the Band-Aid, grabbed it, and yanked it off.

"Ouch. A little passive-aggression there, Phil?" said Edie.

"Sissy, that couldn't have hurt. The cut is tiny, looks clean, should heal okay," said Phil.

"It's my skin that you just yanked off; I'll judge when it hurts. The whole department concurs with your assessment." Edie directed her attention to Sera. "How well did you know Phil's dad?" She remembered how cozy they looked in the old yearbooks she had seen.

"We went out a few times. How was your day?"

"Backlog of paperwork and cases," said Edie.

"Heard Harold told you to find Sage," said Sera.

"He's not the only one who is demanding it," said Edie, wondering how Sera had found out.

"Edie, Edie."

Edie turned around to see Lisa VandenHuevel coming up the driveway with Matilda and Brandon, who always seemed to be his big sister's shadow.

"Edie," said Lisa, "I saw you drive past, thought this would be a good time for you to talk to my kids. Hear what they have to say about Sage. You know, before everything goes cold. That's what they call it on TV, isn't it?"

Edie counted to ten before she spoke. "Has Deputy Johnson talked with you and the kids?"

"Yes, and he did a fine job, but with you on the case, I thought you'd like to hear it firsthand."

"This isn't the best setting for that, Lisa. I'd like to talk with each of them separately when we can have more privacy," said Edie, attempting to balance diplomacy with directness.

Lisa didn't take the not-so-subtle hint. Neither did Phil or Sera. None of them moved an inch.

"Oh, this is just fine, I'm sure they aren't going to tell you anything different from what they told Deputy Johnson. Isn't that right, kids?" Lisa gave her children a meaningful look.

Then why am I going through this? thought Edie, sitting on the step and reviewing what little facts she knew about Sage's disappearance before she began the interview.

"Matilda, Brandon, you two sit on either side of Mrs. Best," Lisa instructed.

Let it go, let it go, thought Edie.

Phil smiled as he stepped off the porch while Sera stood up and then leaned against the door to make way for the kids.

"I'd like to talk with Matilda and Brandon separately," said Edie.

"That's okay, Edie, they aren't going to tell you anything different, are you kids?"

Matilda and Brandon shook their heads no.

"Well, kids, what can you tell me about Sage?"

"She's nice," said Matilda.

"She's been coming up here a lot since she got her driver's license. Sometimes that's okay, but not when her and Matilda gang up on me," said Brandon.

"When did you last see Sage?"

"Sunday," both kids said in unison.

"Do you remember the time?"

"Not exactly, I think it was after lunch," said Matilda.

"Yeah, we ate lunch, and then Mattie drove me to my friend's place in Columbus," said Brandon.

"When I got home, Sage was gone," Matilda said.

"That's what they told Deputy Johnson and what I remember," said Lisa. "I wasn't here when she left, but called Lindsey, Sage's mom, my older sister, as soon as I got home to give her a head's up."

"Head's up for what?"

"That Sage was on her way home, so Lindsey could figure out the time when Sage would be home."

Edie went back to quizzing Matilda and Brandon. "Anything different about Sage this visit?"

"Her hair was shorter," said Brandon.

Matilda shook her head no.

"Where are my manners? Thank-you for paying for Sage's haircut, Edie. I don't know where my brain was. All I could think about was how disappointed her parents would be when they saw how she cut her hair. I should have thought of sending her to Carole," said Lisa.

"Anything else you kids want to add?" asked Edie.

Matilda and Brandon shook their heads.

"The same thing they told that deputy, but I thought you needed to hear directly from them," said Lisa.

"Okay, I'll talk with Deputy Johnson and see what he's found," said Edie.

"I've got a few things to say," shouted Harold from the end of the drive. "Saw you drive past my house, Edie, decided to come talk to you. Then I saw Lisa and the kids walking this way, knew they'd be talking with you about that little girl."

Edie looked up and down the county road that ran in front of her house and spotted the historian striding past the VandenHuevels, waving to her. She knew Troutbeck would have the whole story by suppertime. It would be a major subject in the Troutbeck Chronicles. She put her annoyance on hold and concentrated on the group in front of her. "Harold, what do you have to add?"

"Wondering if you've searched Troutbeck," said Harold.

"No, I haven't."

"What are you waiting for? Get going. You're burning daylight," said Harold.

"Tomorrow," said Edie. "I'm waiting for tomorrow."

"Do it now," demanded Harold. "The minutes are adding up, fast."

Edie noticed that everyone was pressing closer around her. "I'll need to review Johnson's notes," she told them.

Phil stepped in. "Sorry, everyone, but Edie and I don't have time right now," he said. "We're supposed to have supper with Hank and Aunt Jill and neither of us are ready."

The Troutbeck crowd moved closer to Edie.

"Tell you what I can do tonight, I'll drive through Troutbeck on the way to Aunt Jill's," said Edie. "Does that satisfy everyone for now?"

Everyone's shoulders relaxed. They nodded their approval of Edie's plan and then they took a step back from Edie.

"You got to know that I am not officially on this case because I'm closely connected to Sage. But I will be looking into her disappearance," said Edie.

"You'll find her," said Harold. "Mark my word, where her car is, she is; them kids don't wander far from their cars. Never did, never will."

"Edie, we need to get ready, we're already late," Phil reminded her, but he was looking at their neighbors when he spoke.

"Harold, I'll give you a ride home," said Sera, taking the hint. She stepped off the porch, linked arms with Harold, and guided him toward her house.

"Call me when you find something," said Lisa, pulling her kids behind her.

The historian was the last one standing on Edie's lawn. "Sorry I didn't get here earlier, Edie. I saw Harold walking this way and thought I should follow him, wanted to know what was happening. My God, I didn't know my fellow Troutbeckians were so demanding. What are you going to do, Edie?"

"What I told the group I would do—to begin with, I'll drive through Troutbeck tonight for a quick look to see if anything is out of place there," Edie replied.

"You know it isn't. When this is all over, will you come and talk with me? I want to know it all." The historian turned to leave and then turned back to Edie. "You sure have made this town interesting to write about. Until you came, most of what I wrote was about the everyday stuff like births, deaths, marriages, divorces. You made writing exciting again. Whoever reads these Chronicles in the future will have a good time."

Edie and Phil stood on the porch and waved the historian goodbye.

"Boy, they're a pushy bunch," said Phil. "Looked like they were ganging up on you, seemed as if they were turning into a mob. Didn't know what they'd do to you."

"I've seen it before. And yes, this bump-in-the-road town seemed sweet and innocent when we first moved out here. Goes to show that looks can fool you."

"Are you really going to look for Sage?"

"Do I have a choice?"

"We always have choices."

"Sure we do, mine are: look for Sage or be lynched."

"They wouldn't do that."

"You saw the little mob action that just happened. Because one girl has gone missing, their world has been turned upside down. These people need to make their community predictable again. They need to be made whole again. Or they will do something to ease their anxieties."

"So, you're going to do this?" asked Phil.

"Looks that way. Unless you want to move."

"Can't. My business is here. Guess I'll stay and watch as the legend of Edie Swift grows," said Phil.

"Next you'll be putting me in skimpy, splashy outfits," said Edie.

"What you were wearing at breakfast would be fine with me," said Phil.

Chapter 19

†

Edie rode shotgun as Phil drove slowly through Troutbeck. She waved at Carole, who kindly waved back. Edie knew that nothing would be out of place in the town, but she kept an eagle eye out anyway. The open garages held the usual: rakes, lawn mowers; kids' play stuff—nothing out of place. Edie could identify that each of the cars parked on the lawns belonged to the homeowner. She even knew the cars of the people visiting Troutbeck—nothing was where it shouldn't be.

"Tyler Wolfrum has a new car," Edie observed.

"Yeah, a Plymouth Horizon, he's been looking for one to fix up. Boy, that little car would go through anything, best one I've ever had. Hope Vanessa knew about before he bought it; heard she was hoping he'd a Jaguar to fix up," said Phil.

"We'll get the story behind it soon," said Edie.

"Have to stop and see if he needs any help in restoring it."

"Is a Horizon the first car you owned?"

"Yes."

"Boys and their cars, how did any girl get attention?"

"I'll show you later."

They finished the short drive through Troutbeck and then headed out to Hank's.

"Think Troutbeck got the message that I'm on the job?" asked Edie.

"Yup. Super Detective Edie and her trusty sidekick Phil are on the job."

"Then drive on, my good man, drive on."

"Where to?"

"Pick up our baby."

Aunt Jill and Hillary were playing in the yard when Edie and Phil drove in. Hillary tripped on the uneven ground as she rushed toward the car. Aunt Jill scooped up Hillary before she reached the car. In less than a second, Edie was out of the car and standing next to Aunt Jill and Hillary. Aunt Jill handed Hillary to Edie. Mother and daughter shared hugs and kisses until Hillary saw Phil get out of the car. She wiggled her way out of her mother's arms, then ran toward Phil, who gathered her in his arms

"A daddy's girl already," said Edie.

"You shouldn't stay away so long," Phil replied, returning Hillary's kisses.

Aunt Jill cut in, "I was hoping you'd be here earlier. I wanted to take a walk with you, Edie."

"Can we fit it in now?"

"Am I invited or is there something you two need to discuss?" asked Phil.

"Phil, you're always welcome. If you want to hear three women gabbing, come along," replied Aunt Jill.

"Who's the third?" said Phil.

"Yesenia, maybe," replied Aunt Jill.

"Is she the girl you were telling me about?" asked Edie.

"Yes, thought she could point out where that car always stops."

"Where is she?"

"Right now, milking."

"Can she get someone to take her place?"

"Maybe, I did ask Hank to find a replacement for her at this milking, but the worker situation is pretty tight for Hank right now. I've been wondering if he's going to ask me to help out in the barn."

"Do you know the site Yesenia talked about?"

"The general area."

"Is it safe for Hillary to come?"

"Sure, but someone has to carry her. I don't

want her to get the idea she can be down by the road by herself."

"Sounds like you don't need me around," Phil said. "Think I'll take this princess to look at the cows." Daddy and daughter went to the milking parlor in search of Hank. And Edie followed Aunt Jill down the drive.

Aunt Jill led Edie down the long gravel drive to County Line Road, turned east until reaching the corner woodlot, then turned south.

"Have you set a day for you and me to get together?" asked Aunt Jill.

"It slipped my mind."

"Don't doubt that, you have your plate full. How does Sunday sound?"

"This Sunday?"

"Yes, Phil usually doesn't have anything to do, he can watch Hillary."

"Sounds like you've got a plan."

"Yes, it's about giving you a break."

"Sunday it is. Tell me again what Yesenia told you," Edie said.

"Yessie told me that one day when she was walking this road, a white car pulled up behind her and stopped, and she crossed to the other side of the road, and then she came back to the farm. She says that the car has been here, in the same place, same time, and she thinks the same driver, for the past few mornings. She tells me that she doesn't walk that way anymore."

"Has she told anyone else about this car?"

"I don't know."

"Why did she tell you?"

"I am friends with both of you."

"What difference does that make?"

"I think she's looking for some help. She knows what you do for a living and she trusts me. I think I must be a mother substitute for her or something like that."

"That seems to be one of your specialties."

"Edie, I've told her about our talk. She knows that you're a cop and haven't turned her into ICE yet. She says that she will trust you because Hank and I do. She's also of the opinion that you don't take shit from nobody."

"I don't know the girl from Adam; how'd she get that idea?"

"Really, Edie, you don't know?"

"Know what?"

"How other people see you?"

"Whatever people see in me isn't deliberate on my part. I have no grand plan. I am me. So, tell me, Aunt Jill, what do people see when they look at me?"

"You are a take-charge, no-nonsense kind of person. People instinctively know that they can trust you. I think you've always had those qualities.

They became more apparent after your Florida escapade. I think you became more defined after you returned. Your friends noticed it, and a few adults did too."

"You did."

"I'm different."

"Yes, you are." What do you say after the adult who has guided you through life just made you her equal, if not put you on a pedestal? "Hmmm" was all that Edie could come up with on short notice. "I'm going to be looking around here a while. Your choice to stay here or go back to the farm," said Edie, focusing on the job her aunt had asked her to do.

"I'd rather stay; I'd like to watch how a real detective works."

"Okay, but you have to stay behind me and at the edge of the road. I don't want you unknowingly messing up the area."

"What are you looking for?"

"Nothing in particular, I'll know it when I see it."

"Give me some concrete examples."

"In this case I can't give you a specific until I see it."

"That sounds like gobbledygook."

"Yes, it does. I'll try to phrase that better. Aunt Jill, most of us don't think about the moment we live in. We just live it. One minute blurs into another, habit takes over. My job is to step into another's person's life and for a moment to look over that person's shoulders and figure out what they were doing at any given moment."

"Such as," said Aunt Jill.

"Let's say this man was sitting alone in the car watching Hank's farm; maybe he's been here a few times and nobody's noticed him. He recognizes a few things in the area; beginning to understand what happens on a daily basis, it's become routine for him. So, now he's alone, comfortable with the area, he relaxes. When we're alone, content, most of us fall back on routine—we just do what we usually do. So, while he was watching Hank's farm, what did he do? Eat breakfast and throw the wrappers in the ditch? Did he chew gum and toss out the wrapper and gum into the ditch—just one of those things or neither? Did he drop a pop or beer can in the ditch? Or did he just sit there?"

"Never thought about the habits we develop."

"I do, every day," said Edie, focusing on the ground around her.

It looked as if Edie was meandering as she walked east on County Line Road from the shoulder into the ditch, then back again, repeating her actions on the other side of the road. But there was a method. It paid off when she meandered along Shoe Road. An empty can of chewing tobacco. From her back pocket, she pulled a paper bag, opened it, and then, using a twig, pushed the can into it.

"Where'd that come from?" asked Aunt Jill.

"What?"

"Why are you carrying a paper bag in your pocket?"

"Don't know. Maybe I was going to make it into a puppet for Hillary or pick up trash in the car. Or just in case, like now. Mostly from habit, I guess."

"Think that tin is important?"

"No way of knowing," said Edie.

"Can't you check it for fingerprints or something?"

"If it can be retrieved, do what with that information?"

"Start an investigation. Search for the person who threw it there."

"Other than littering, no crime or any suspicious activity has been reported as far as I understand," said Edie.

"Aren't you going to write up a report?"

"I haven't seen anything but an empty tin of chew. Probably only a litterbug. Maybe it's someone around here who chews tobacco. Has anyone reported a suspicious or an unlawful activity to the police?"

"Yesenia will."

"You told me this morning that she was uncomfortable talking to the police."

"Me. I'll be the one reporting the suspicious activity."

"I'll write up an official report tomorrow," said Edie. "And start running the plates."

"How long is this going to take?"

"Depends on how far I've got to dig and what other cases I have to investigate."

At Hank's driveway, Edie stopped. "Aunt Jill?"

Aunt Jill had kept on walking. She stopped when Edie called to her again. "Did you find something else?"

"No. Just wondering…"

Aunt Jill walked back to Edie. "Wondering about what?"

"Marriage."

"Has Phil asked you to marry him?"

"Multiple times."

"And you've said yes?"

"Always found a reason not to. Been wondering if there is a reason to say yes."

"Why are you asking me? I've never been married."

"I know that, thought you might have given it some consideration over the years."

"Not much. Never found a reason to think about it."

"Were you ever asked?"

"By a few people, always said no. Don't know

if I objected to marriage or the people doing the asking."

"Got any advice for me?"

"Good luck. It's your decision. You have to live with whatever you do."

Chapter 20

†

In the early morning, after a restless night, Edie sat in the family room, which now looked like a toy store, hoping to catch a breeze while she assessed what she had let herself be led into. She set her mug of coffee on the wood stove and reviewed the explosion of problems that were popping up around her. Sage was missing and Troutbeck residents were demanding she get involve. Aunt Jill wanted her to help an undocumented worker with an unknown problem. Phil's trucks seemed to be a target of somebody. And Hillary was becoming a toddler. It used to be that she came home from work and shut the door on the world's problem. Now, when she came home from work, the problems flew in the window instead of staying out. How did she get dragged into this stuff? Edie contemplated Hillary's baby picture. "It's you, you did this. Since it takes a village to raise a child, I found one for you, and they've assigned the village police role to me. And as long as I live here, I guess that role is mine—whether I like it or not." She rose from her chair and went to make breakfast.

At work, Edie typed up Aunt Jill's complaint, started the search for the RBR license plate—a huge number of possibilities were generated. Edie hit print and watched the office printer spew out paper after paper. This was going to be one tedious job.

The print job went on and on; there were other things that needed to be done besides watching a print job. She made sure the printer had lots of paper before going over to place the chewing tobacco can into evidence. Ben Harris's desk was ringed with cops. It was obvious that Ben was telling one of his family stories. She joined the group—Ben's stories were too good to miss.

"Got any more, Ben?" someone in that gaggle of deputies asked.

"There is one from a few years back, happened during the ice storm," said Ben.

"Could use a good winter story these days, it might help cool me off," said one of the deputies gathered around Ben's desk.

"Haven't had an ice storm for a long time," someone said.

"Really, seems like yesterday to me. Anyway, during this ice storm, my cousin..." Ben began, again.

"Which one?"

"Take your pick, there's lots of them. Anyway..." Ben stopped and looked to see if anyone was thinking of interrupting him. He began, again. "Anyone else want to chime in here?" he asked. "Okay, then, I've got the floor. The morning after the ice storm, my cousin decided to be a good neighbor. Guess he figured the mess in his own yard would be there when he came back or he was looking for someone to give him lunch. He's such a moocher. Anyway, he fueled up his chainsaw, made sure it was in working condition, and went out to trim his neighbors' branches. He went from one neighbor to another cutting the downed limbs into chunks of usable firewood. Then he came to a neighbor who wanted a whole tree cut down 'cause most of the branches were busted up, so my cousin made his calculations as to which way to fell the tree and during his last cut of that tree a gust of wind swept that tree in the other direction, taking out the garage and the car parked in it. It almost took out my cousin, too.

"Sorry about that," said my cousin, picking himself out of the snow.

"Well," said the neighbor, "looks like the storm claimed its last victim. I needed a new car anyway."

"My cousin decided to quit being a Good Samaritan, and went home. Decided it was time to cut the branches that were down in his own yard. While he was cutting them up, he kept looking at the tree in his front yard; seemed to him that the tree was leaning too much. The more he looked at it, the more it leaned. He determined that it had to come down, right then and there, before it caused problems. So he makes his calculations, started his saw, and began taking down one of the lower branches. The branch came down on the electrical lines. He took out the power to half the town."

"Good story to remind us what winter is all about," said one of the cops.

"I think I can make it through the rest of summer just thinking about it," said another.

The crowd thinned down to Ben and Edie.

"Which part of your story was true?" asked Edie.

"Take your pick," Ben replied. "Got something for me?"

Edie handed over the brown paper bag containing the empty tin of chew.

"What's the story behind this?" Ben asked as he filled out the paperwork.

"An incomplete one for now. My aunt filed a complaint. Just beginning to look into it for her.

Found the tin in a ditch, don't know how long it's been there. Can you check it out?" She started to walk back to her department, but returned to Ben's desk.

"Anything else, Edie?"

"There's something I've been wondering about. Are you the only smart one in your family?"

"Why do you ask?"

"Seems to me as if every one of your relatives you tell us about is one sandwich short of a picnic," said Edie.

"I'll tell you something about my family."

"What?"

"I get to tell the stories."

Edie looked at the clock; it had been an hour since she had begun the work of eliminating cars with RBR license plate from the list she had generated. Damn, she needed some TV cops to help her. By now the bad guys would have been identified, caught, court testimony given, jury decided the perp's fate, and the now guilty person would be on their way to prison. And the world would once again be safe for democracy. She looked at the clock; she'd wasted five minutes in the fantasy of TV Copland. She went back to work.

"Edie." Was it her imagination or was someone

trying to get her attention? "Edie." She finally looked up. It was Detective Fitzgerald.

"Sorry, Luke, what can I do for you?"

"Nothing, just got some info on that girl from your town."

Edie closed her eyes. Damn, not only was she Troutbeck's superhero, now she owned the town. Maybe it was a mistake to move from Madison. "What did you find?"

"Her car was found near the UW campus."

"Have her parents been notified?"

"Of course. Madison Police are questioning area residents about the car and girl."

"Any security cameras in the area?"

"None. Don't think any of this will pan out, you know what students are like. They move every year and aren't at home most of the time. They don't really know who lives in the neighborhood because everyone is new, but there's always a chance someone may remember her."

"Any sign of a struggle occurring in the car?"

"Going to check the car now."

"Who's going with you?"

"Ben."

"Should be fun, stories seem to be spilling out of him today. Keep me informed?"

"Yes. What are you going to tell your neighbor?"

"Nothing, that's your job or you can assign it to Johnson. If you've got a few minutes, I've read the reports you and Johnson filed on Sage Staley, I've got the facts. Now I want to hear about the soft stuff, what impressions of the girl you got from your interviews," replied Edie.

"Can't get a handle on the girl. The aunt gives the impression that the girl was rebellious. From what the cousin says, the girl seems like an ordinary teenager."

"What's your take on Matilda?"

"Calm, sensible, eager to help. What's yours, Edie?"

"Same thing or I wouldn't have let her near my kid. Mind if I talk with Matilda?"

"Thought you already had."

"I did, but half of Troutbeck listened in on the conversation. And now I'd like to talk to her minus the audience."

"Go ahead; it would be good to have another set of eyes on this. Keep me informed?"

"Sure."

After Luke left, thoughts of Sage crowded everything else out of her brain. Edie went through the scenarios of what could have happened: Sage was abducted somewhere between Troutbeck and Madison, she was a runaway, committed suicide, death by foul play, forced into the sex trade, kidnapping, became part of a cult. There were lots of possibilities; she only reviewed the worst-case scenarios. She had lots of experience with those; at one time or another during Edie's career, each of those possibilities had turned into a significant case. None of them turned out well.

She slammed her fist on her desk; Edie couldn't take the paperwork anymore. Action—she needed to move this case forward. Everyone in the room turned to watch her as she swept a stack of papers into her desk drawer, shoved the rest into the shred bin, and then strode out of the room.

As she waited for the slowest elevator in the universe, Edie counted her steps, four steps to the wall, and four steps back to the front of the elevator. Then four steps to the hallway and four steps back to the elevator. All the counting helped focus her thoughts. Instead of telling the assholes of the world to stop being assholes, she could focus on the interviews she was about to have with two young women from Troutbeck. If only that damned elevator would show up.

For a Thursday night, the traffic out of Madison was heavy. All the way home, Edie damned the drivers, and the perpetual road construction that was slowing her progress. Didn't they know she had a job to do?

When Edie turned onto the county road toward

home, she saw a moving van pull away from the old corner store. Everybody in Troutbeck would be watching the activity at the old store. For a moment, she considered backing up and driving around the country block to avoid passing the VandenHuevels, but that would take her five miles out of her way. Luck was with her; she didn't see any cars in the drive and no one was outside. At home, she hotfooted it into the house, changed into shorts and T-shirt, and called Phil to let him know her plans. After peeking out the door to see if any Troutbeckian was in sight, she sprinted to the car to pick up Hillary at Hank's. She hoped no one had seen her drive home and would stop by for an update. Maybe she could go about her own business.

Chapter 21

†

Aunt Jill sat under the spreading elm tree, one of the few in the area which had not died from Dutch Elm disease, watching a Mexican girl chasing after a laughing Hillary.

Edie sat down next to Aunt Jill waiting for her daughter to notice her.

"How was your day?" asked Aunt Jill.

"Not bad."

"Must be nice to say that after the week you've had. Have you had a chance to work on finding that white car?"

"Started, but with only a partial plate, it may take a few more days."

"The girl playing with Hillary is Yesenia, the girl I've been telling you about."

"Will she talk to me?"

"I think she will. She understands a lot of

English, but isn't comfortable speaking it. Says she doesn't want to sound stupid."

"I know some Spanish."

"I'm learning some, being able to talk to the workers comes in handy," Aunt Jill said and she called to the young woman. "Yesenia, ven aquí, por favor."

Edie did a quick assessment of the girl as she walked to Aunt Jill. The girl was young, maybe still a teenager. About five foot one. Black hair, a single thick braid down her back. A solid body, not fat. Her gait was short, more like baby steps.

Yesenia picked up Hillary, walked to Aunt Jill, and handed Hillary to her. The little girl squirmed out of Aunt Jill's arms and into her mother's.

"Yessie, this is my niece, Edie. I've told you about her, she works for the sheriff's office."

Yessie's eyes widened, and she backed away from Aunt Jill.

Aunt Jill stood up, took Yessie's hand, and pulled her into a hug.

"Yesenia, you trust me—confías en mi?" whispered Aunt Jill.

Yessie nodded.

"Edie está aquí para ayudarte. Te lo prometo. Ella quiere hacerte unas preguntas." Aunt Jill released Yessie from the hug, but continued to hold her hand.

"Me llevarán?" Yessie softly asked Aunt Jill.

169

Edie set Hillary on the ground and stood up. "No." Next to the young woman, Edie looked and felt like a giant. "Tiá Jill me contó acerca del carro, pero quiero escucharlo viniendo de ti. De qué color era?"

"Blanco."

"Cuántas puertas tenía?"

"Cuatro."

"Era nuevo?"

"Viejo, tenía óxido en las puertas."

"Viste las placas?"

"Tenía sólo una en la parte de atrás."

"Recuerdas el numero de la placa?"

"Sólo RBR."

"Viste de qué estado venía?"

"Wisconsin."

"Cómo puedes estar segura?"

"Puedo leer inglés, bueno, un poquito. Además, tenía un dibujo de una granja."

"Cuántas veces has visto ese carro?"

"Dos o tres... no recuerdo."

"Dónde estaba el carro?"

"Allí." Yesenia pointed to the grove of trees at the far corner of the farm.

"A qué hora del día lo viste?"

"En la mañana."

"Dónde estaba cuando lo viste?"

Yesenia spoke to the ground. "Mirando las flores. Siempre voy al bosque a buscar flores."

"Porqué?"

"No me gusta el olor de las vacas todo el día."

"Quién manejaba el carro?" asked Edie.

Yesenia still stared at the ground.

"Era un hombre o una mujer quién manejaba?"

"Un hombre," Yesenia whispered, her head bent.

"Joven o viejo?"

"Viejo." Yesenia's shoulders started to shake.

"Viejo cómo yo?"

Yesenia shook her head no.

"Viejo cómo la tía Jill?"

Yesenia nodded her head. She sobbed.

Aunt Jill pulled Yesenia into her arms and held her tight.

Yesenia fought her way out of Aunt Jill's arms and ran toward the barns.

Edie and Aunt Jill stared after the retreating Yesenia, then at each other.

Hank, carrying Hillary, joined them. "Found this little darling near the barns, thought you might be missing her." He handed Hillary to Edie. "What did you two do to make my Yesenia cry?"

"Nothing, it was what she was telling us," said Aunt Jill.

"It was what she wasn't saying that made her cry," said Edie. "I think I know where this investigation is pointing, but I need that girl to talk to me, to confirm it—I can only go so far with my intuition. Goddamn the people who are making her scared to ask for help. Goddamn the witch hunts of immigrants. They have every right to be protected by us. They have a right to be made whole again. Goddamn it, I'm here to help people in need, not send them into hiding. Goddamn them all," said Edie.

"That's a lot of Goddamns," said Hank.

"What else can you say when idiocy rules the day?" said Edie.

Chapter 22

†

It was suppertime and Phil hadn't called back, a sure indication that it was going to be a long night for him and Edie. Edie fixed a plate of food for him and put it in the fridge. While Hillary ate, she called Phil. "Hey."

"Sorry, can't talk now," said Phil.

"When are you coming home?"

"Don't know. Not for a while," said Phil and hung up.

Edie stared at the phone. "He hung up on me! What the fuck! Damn it, Phil, I need you to watch Hillary so I can talk to Matilda. Sorry, Hillary, don't repeat anything I just said."

Hillary ignored her and smashed her spoon into the squash, sending it flying all over herself and the kitchen and Edie.

"When, little girl, will you stop playing with

your food, and when will you be able to stay alone? I can see that's not going to happen tonight. How would you like to come to Matilda's house with me? Eat what's left of the squash on your plate. When you are done I'll clean up you and me, then we'll go see Matilda," said Edie as she cleaned gobs of the yellow stuff off the floor, the fridge, and cupboards.

Hillary smashed her spoon into what was left of the squash, scattering the food in places Edie had just cleaned.

Edie rinsed the rag and began again.

Edie and Hillary stood at the VandenHuevels' front door.

Lisa answered their knock. "Hi, Edie, and you too, Hillary. Hope you weren't standing here long, I didn't hear you knock until now; I was back in the kitchen cleaning up after supper. Do you have any news about Sage?"

"Her car was found in Madison. The police are asking the local residents about it." Edie was surprised that no one had told Lisa.

"See, I knew you'd get things done, thank-you." Lisa invited them in, then shut and locked the door.

"I was hoping to talk to Matilda again."

"I don't know if she has anything different to say, but if it would make a difference, I'm sure that she would be happy to talk with you."

"May I talk with her now?"

"I'm so sorry, she isn't here. She's spending a few days with friends in Columbus. I wasn't certain if I should let her go, but Brad said it would be good for her to get away from all the doom and gloom around here. Said it would do her good to do something normal with her friends. You know how girls are, hanging around, gossiping and getting in their last lazy days before school."

No, Edie wanted to reply, she and her friends didn't have lazy days—they worked hard, and played the same way. "I'm off tomorrow, would Matilda be willing to come home and talk to me for a bit or maybe I could go to her friend's house?"

"I'm certain she'd be happy to, but I've found that when she's with her friends, she doesn't answer my calls. She must turn her cell phone off. I never thought a young girl would ever turn off her phone, but maybe she doesn't need the phone when she's surrounded with friends. Sorry she isn't here right now, but Matilda will be back tomorrow night. Why don't you come by then?"

"I'll see you and Matilda then. Thanks."

With Hillary asleep, the news over, Edie was flipping through the TV channels when Phil walked in.

"You're up," said Phil.

"You sound disappointed."

"I knew you'd want to talk, but I'm too tired for that."

"And dirty. Go hit the shower."

Phil headed for the bathroom.

"Drop those clothes in the laundry room first, then go shower."

Phil looked down; dirt and grease hid his clothes. He untied his work boots, dropped his clothes on the floor, and walked to the bathroom.

"Are you hungry? I've got supper waiting for you."

"Picked up a sandwich on the way home."

Edie picked Phil's clothes off the floor; he looked as if he'd had a hard day and needed a little kindness. She put his clothes in the laundry sink to soak. Stood outside the locked bathroom, did a quick cleanup of the room after Phil finished, and then she joined him in bed. Phil looked as if he was sleeping. She rolled next to him and gave him a nudge. "Why so late?"

"Tell you tomorrow." Phil turned away from Edie.

"Can you give me the short version now?"

"Max's truck got paint bombed." Phil pulled a pillow over his head.

The short version didn't sit well with Edie—it wasn't enough—but Phil was already asleep. Edie couldn't tell if he was faking it or not.

Chapter 23

†

Despite her restless night Edie was up early making breakfast.

Hillary was dropping pieces of her waffle on the floor when Phil sat down. She offered him a piece. He gobbled it up.

Edie pulled a plate of bacon and waffles from the oven, then put a scoop of scrambled eggs on it before placing it in front of Phil.

He looked at the plate and looked at Edie. "What are you planning?"

"Nothing. Why do you ask?"

"Looks like I'm being fattened up for something."

"Can't I just cook on my day off?"

"Okay, I'll take you at your word. But I still think something's up."

"Now tell me about what happened yesterday with Max."

"I'm surprised you didn't hear."

"I was in the office most of the morning, never heard a request for all hands. If one was issued, it was after I left and got busy with other cases. Now, tell me what happened."

"You know that my trucks have been hit with water balloons a few times, well, this time Max's truck got hit with paint-filled balloons. The whole windshield was splattered with paint. He went into the ditch, smashed up the truck. He was lucky; he walked away with just scrapes and bruises. After he finished talking to the deputies, I drove him to the emergency room to make sure he was okay, and then drove him home. Then, after I pulled the truck out of the ditch, I went looking for a replacement."

"For Max or the truck?"

"The truck, Max quit. It'll take some time finding a replacement driver. Don't know which one is pissing me off more, getting a new truck or having to find a new driver."

"Is he okay?"

"Physically, yes, mentally, don't know if he ever was. But he was pretty shaken up."

"Who's taking over his route?"

"Me, I'm the boss. I'll be pulling some long days when the new truck is delivered. I won't be able to take Hillary for a few days; we'll have to make arrangements for her care. Maybe my mother can move in here for a few days."

"Or maybe Aunt Jill can pick up a couple more days. How much is this going to set you back?"

"I'll know after my insurance guy gets me an estimate today."

"That story was short, why couldn't you have told me last night?"

"The long version included a lot of swearing. What about you?"

"Lots of work to catch up on. Was wondering if you could watch Hillary today?"

"I knew it, that's why you made all this food."

"No. I made it with love. Take a bite, you'll taste that ingredient."

Phil tasted the waffle. "Mmmm, delicious. My mother always told me to marry someone who could cook. Marry me."

"Your mother reference doesn't do a thing for me. And I doubt that she ever uses the word good to describe me. So...can you watch Hillary?"

"After work I can. What are you going to do?"

"Run."

Edie filled the morning by playing with Hillary. For every tower of blocks that Edie built, Hillary knocked it down, laughed, and handed the blocks to Edie so she could start the building project again. "Little one, isn't it time for your nap? This mama sure could use you taking one."

But the tower building continued until Edie had enough. "Sorry, sweetie, but I can't do this anymore. I need something more than playing with blocks, and it's obvious you're not ready for a nap. So, I am going for a run and you get to keep me company on that run."

Edie slathered sunscreen over Hillary and herself, tied a floppy hat on her daughter, put one of Phil's baseball caps on herself, secured Hillary in the stroller, and headed down the road into Troutbeck. "I remember when running was easy. Back in the days when I didn't have to take the kitchen sink with me. Damn, I'm getting old, that kitchen sink thingy could have been said by my grandmother. Maybe that's where I heard it. Remind me to tell you about your Great Grandmother Swift when you're older, way older. Maybe when I'm an old lady and understand her." They were almost to the corner store.

"Hey, girlie," someone shouted.

Edie kept running.

"Hey, you with the stroller."

She knew the voice meant her, but Edie looked around anyway in the hope of seeing someone else on the road. No luck, all she saw was a car passing through Troutbeck. There was no means of escape; she'd have to respond. Edie looked around for the person who was shouting at her.

"Up here, you dope."

Edie looked up; a white-haired woman on the second floor of the old corner store was staring back at her. "My name's Edie. What's yours?"

"Grizzly Jack. Do you live in this speed trap?"

"Yes, last house down..."

"Good for you. I thought this town was only a speed trap. Now I find it's full of busybodies and vagrants. I'm going to let that realtor have an earful, if she ever answers my calls."

"I don't understand."

"A busybody showed up at my door this morning asking questions; that meddler must have been trained by the FBI."

"That would be Troutbeck's self-appointed historian who talked to you. Wants to chronicle everything that happens in Troutbeck. Shows up at all the town's funerals, weddings, and such...you're the newest thing happening around here."

"Well, the historian can stay out of my business."

"Good luck with that," Edie whispered to Hillary. Then she yelled up to Grizzly Jack. "You said something about vagrants."

"To steal a quote from one of the three bears, someone's been sleeping in my house."

"How do you know?"

"Bag full of garbage neatly tied up in my kitchen and a couple of diet pops in my fridge."

"Can I take a look?"

"What for? You in cahoots with that nosy neighbor?"

"Would like to see for myself if anything is out of place."

"Are you calling me a liar? I've already told you what I found. Trash and pop."

"But there might be something more to see."

"Who are you? The police? I'm telling you, there isn't anything else." The woman slammed the window shut.

"Matter of fact, I am the police," said Edie. Damn, thought Edie, now we've got another foul-mouthed crazy old coot living in Troutbeck, one for each end of town. Behind her came the sound of a door slamming shut. She turned around; the old woman was walking toward her carrying a garbage bag and two cans of pop.

"Here you go, girlie. Do what you want with them," said Grizzly Jack, holding out the bag and cans to Edie.

Edie took possession of them. "Thanks."

"Why are you so eager to look through other people's trash? You a cop or something?"

"I am."

"Then find out who's been in my house."

They were interrupted by Harold Acker. "Hi, Edie," Harold bent over to tickle Hillary's toes. "Morning, little darling." He stood up and stretched. "Was on my way home from visiting my Mamie when I saw you standing here, came over to see what progress you've made in finding that missing girl."

"Still checking out leads," said Edie.

"Not to worry, it's early yet, I suppose. I know you'll come up with something," said Harold.

"Thanks for the confidence. Harold, have you met our newest neighbor, Grizzly Jack? Ms. Jack, this is Harold Acker, he lives at the other end of town."

"What are you looking at, old man?"

"You, I was thinking you might kinda look nice, if you smiled."

"Old man, I'll smile when I want to. I'm not your mother, and I'm not inviting you into my bed."

"Wouldn't accept the invite."

"Wasn't making one." Grizzly Jack turned and walked back to her house, slamming the door.

"Just what this town needs, another cranky old lady to deal with." Harold turned to Edie. "What are you gawking at? Do something. Go find that girl. You're wasting my money standing there." Harold stomped across the road to resume his walk home.

Edie was left holding the bag and two cans of pop. "I don't run a twenty-four-hour cop shop. Hillary, I think it's time to find us a new home, the foul-mouthed old people around here are multiplying." She shoved the bag and pop cans under the stroller and finished her run to Phil's shop.

He wasn't there—damn, just when she needed a sane adult to talk to.

When Phil walked in the door that night, Edie walked out. As she passed him, she told him what he needed to know, "Supper's on the table. Hillary's in the living room. I need a run. See you later."

"Love you too," he yelled after her.

Her running plan was to head west out of Troutbeck, but those plans crumbled when she saw Carole sitting on Bridget Briggs' porch drinking beer with her...and they saw her. They waved for her to join them.

"One of those beers for me?" asked Edie.

"Thought you didn't drink," said Carole.

"Only when I'm on duty or when I have Hillary or when I'm the designated driver for my drunken friends. So...do you have a beer for me?"

"Sorry, didn't know you were coming, only brought two bottles, a root beer for Bridget, and a real one for me," said Carole.

"When did Ray start making root beer?" asked Edie.

"This summer," replied Carole.

"It's pretty good, hope he makes more. How about sharing a bit of gossip with us?" asked Bridget.

"What's the topic?" asked Edie.

"Our new neighbor," said Bridget.

"We haven't met her, have you?" Carole asked.

"Yes. Surprised you two haven't welcomed her to town yet. We chatted for a bit," Edie paused. "That isn't what happened, she talked at me. No, that isn't right, she growled at me."

"Juicy, give us the particulars," said Carole.

"Older woman, around seventy, give or take a few years, white hair, and her name is Grizzly Jack," said Edie.

"Did I hear that right? Say the name again," said Carole.

"Grizzly Jack. It fits her," said Edie. "Harold saw us talking, so he came over and I introduced them. They started throwing daggers at each right away. I was going to say like two peas in a pod, but that's rather mild, more like two ogres vying over who gets to tear your head off. And Hillary and I were in the middle."

"Always thought that old people would be sweet and helpful, they should be setting a good example for our children," said Bridget.

"Those two must have been absent from school when that was taught," said Edie.

"Sorry, don't blame everything on our schools. We can't teach everything at school. Some manners and life skills need to be taught at home," said Bridget.

"Fine example those old people are setting for our young 'uns these days," said Carole.

On her way home Edie stopped at the Vanden-Huevels.

Lisa opened the door in midknock. "When I saw you run past earlier, I knew that you'd stop by. Sorry, Matilda isn't home, yet. You know how these girls are, talk, talk, talk—that's all they seem to do. She'll probably be home late. Should I send her down to your place tomorrow morning?"

"Call me first, I'd like to be up and ready for her," said Edie. The real reason she wanted the call was to be fully dressed when she talked to Matilda.

What a strange week, thought Edie on her way home. It was as if she had been hopping from one crisis to the next, but now it seemed calm, and she didn't know what to do. Had the crises dissipated or was she in the calm center? She didn't care. She wanted to lock her door and crawl into bed for a very long sleep. She liked her job; she needed a break from her neighbors.

Chapter 24

†

Someone was pounding on a door. Please let this be a nightmare, thought Edie, struggling out of sleep. It wasn't. It was for real. She reached for her cell; damn it was early, barely into Friday. And the Goddamn pounding still persisted. Would this week never end? Edie got out of bed.

Edie hurried out of her bedroom; she needed to stop that incessant knocking before it woke Hillary. She was halfway to her front door when it dawned on her that it might be better to answer the door with clothes on. Edie went back to her bedroom and pulled on a T-shirt, pants, and bathrobe. She opened her front door. "Quiet, my baby is sleeping, I hope."

"Sorry," said Lisa VandenHuevel. "I wasn't thinking about Hillary. But she's not home and you were the first person I thought of. What am I going to do,

Edie? She's not at home, she's not at her friend's, no one's talking to me, and you've got to help me." Lisa crumpled onto the front step. Edie stepped out of the house and sat down next to Lisa.

"Lisa, I didn't understand any of that. Let's try this. Lisa, I want you to take a deep breath in, then let it out slowly like you're blowing out birthday candles."

Lisa didn't follow Edie's instructions.

"Lisa, breathe with me. We're going to take a deep breath in, then let it out slowly. Breathe with me."

Lisa mimicked Edie.

Edie did the deep breathing exercise two more times and Lisa followed each time. After the third time, a shudder went through Lisa's body, the sobs stopped, but her tears continued to flow. Lisa leaned against Edie, and then put her head in Edie's lap.

What am I coming to? thought Edie. There are only three people I'd let to this, and one of them—Aunt Jill—would never do that. But she did nothing until Lisa seemed to be calming down. "Lisa, do you think you can talk now?"

Lisa nodded.

"Who didn't come home?"

"Matilda."

Edie's heart sank. Her voice remained steady. "Did you call her?"

"Yes. It rang and rang and rang, then it went to

voice mail both times I called. I left voice messages both times, and then I texted her. Matilda never answered any of them."

"Lisa, remember, you told me Matilda turns off her phone when she's with friends. Did you call her friend?"

"No, I called her friend's mother. She said that Matilda wasn't there and hadn't been there. I asked to talk to Zoe, Matilda's friend, but she wouldn't let me—she said everyone in the house was sleeping. Said she'd have Zoe call me as soon as she was up. And then she hung up. She hung up on me! Why? Edie, I didn't know what to do. What should I do?"

It was looking a lot like the old teen con game. Each friend would swear that they would be with another friend and so and so on, a time-honored tactic of divert and distract. Edie had been a master of it as a teen. Matilda probably swore her friend or friends to silence as she built the shell game. Edie knew that oath of silence among friends was almost unbreakable. What was Matilda trying to hide? Lisa's tears were soaking through Edie's bathrobe. "First, come inside while I get dressed." Once inside, Edie led Lisa to the couch, wrapped a throw around her, and set a box of Kleenex next to her. "I'll be back in a moment."

Phil rolled over and watched Edie get dressed. "Who was pounding on the door and where are you going?"

"Lisa. A little quieter, please, she's out on the couch. Matilda's missing. Don't know when I'll be back. Call Aunt Jill or Carole or Sera, if you need help."

"What can I do?" asked Phil, now alert and sitting up.

"First, get dressed, if you want to talk with Lisa. For now, watch Hillary. Maybe take some food down to Lisa's later in the day, she'll be a basket case until we find Matilda—she won't be able to do anything."

"I'll get right on that," said Phil. He got out of bed, kissed Edie. "You've got to find her." Then he pulled on a pair of shorts and a T-shirt before going to talk with Lisa.

Edie went to the bathroom, brushed her teeth, and talked to her image in the mirror. "I know you, you ain't fooling me, and you don't got no superhero badge or uniform. So don't screw this up."

Lisa was crying on Phil's shoulder when Edie walked into the living room. Phil assisted Lisa to her feet and handed her over to Edie.

"Edie, anything else I can do?" asked Phil as he opened the front door for them.

"Keep the lights on for me."

Chapter 25

†

Edie took Lisa's hand and led her home. Brad and Brandon were sitting on the couch in their pajamas. Both looked worried.

"What's wrong?" asked Brad VandenHuevel. Lisa ran to him, buried her head in his shoulder, and cried. He put his arms around her. "I heard Lisa scream, then the next thing I knew the front door was slammed."

"Matilda is not at her friend's house," said Edie.

"Of course not, she's upstairs sleeping," interrupted Brad. "I'm sure of it. She said she'd be home tonight and Matilda always keeps her promise."

Edie shook her head. "Did you see her come in?"

"No, I went to bed before she got home. Matilda's a good girl, she knows the rules," said Brad.

Lisa stopped sobbing for a second. "No, she's not in her room. I checked. Go see for yourself, Brad."

Brad ran upstairs to Matilda's room. "She's not there." Then Brad and Brandon joined Lisa in sobbing.

Edie herded the three to the couch, where they huddled together. She wrapped throws around them, then handed each of them a box of tissues. "Lisa, have you called the police?"

Lisa shook her head no.

Edie phoned 9-1-1, explained the situation, and asked for a deputy to come to the house. Then she went to the kitchen to make warm drinks for the family.

Edie stood watch over the VandenHuevel family. Mostly the three stayed huddled on the couch as they waited for the sheriff's deputy, their hands wrapped around the mugs of hot chocolate Edie had made for them. But Brad couldn't sit still; he was up and down, walking through the house, going upstairs to check in the bedrooms, making a pit stop in the bathroom, then coming to sit on the couch as if to make sure that Lisa and Brandon were still there before he walked through the house again. When Brad left to wander, Brandon moved next to Lisa and was quickly enfolded in her protective blanket.

The knock on the door startled the Vanden-Huevels, and none of them got up from the couch. On the second knock, Edie answered the door. "Hi, Willis," said Edie, after her eyes adjusted to the dark.

"Edie, I didn't expect you here," said Deputy Hannah Willis, as she waited to be invited in.

"I'm not here on official business, the VandenHuevels are neighbors," replied Edie. "Come on in and meet them."

"Will you be taking over the case?" asked Willis, following Edie into the living room.

"No. I'd rather not, Matilda has babysat for me. I think I am too close to this missing girl to be objective."

"I don't know why she keeps telling us that," said Brad.

"It's true, Brad, but I will assist in the case in any way I can," said Edie. "Go ahead with your interview, Deputy Willis."

"I was hoping for a man," said Brad.

"Sorry, sir, if you would like a male deputy, I can request one to come," said Willis. "But it may be another thirty minutes or more before one can get here."

"Brad, if Edie says this deputy is good, she's fine with me," said Lisa, and then looked to Edie for guidance.

"We need to be working on this fast. I am

acquainted with Deputy Willis and she is good, she knows her stuff," said Edie.

Deputy Willis tried to write down everything that Brad and Lisa said. But it was difficult to follow the conversation; once Lisa and Brad started talking, they couldn't be stopped. The conversation ping-ponged between them; they corrected each other, and often talked over each other as the details of Matilda's life spilled out, from birth until her parents discovered that she wasn't in her bed that night.

Detective Swift and Deputy Willis listened respectfully. Deputy Willis finally gave up on taking notes. "Thank-you, you've answered the questions I usually ask. Sounds as if you've been through this before," she said politely.

"We have," said Brad. "Our niece went missing a few days ago. We were practically drilled by the deputies then."

Deputy Willis perked up at that news, and then looked at Edie for help; the only thing Willis got back from Edie was an unreadable stare. "Was that girl missing from here?"

"We're not sure. She spent a few days with us, drove home, and never made it," said Brad. "We've been told that Sage's car was found in Madison a day or so ago."

"Edie's working on finding her, too," said Lisa.

"Good to have lots of eyes on the case," said Willis.

"That is exactly what Edie says," Lisa replied. "Brad, I think we can trust Deputy Willis."

"Do you have a recent photo of Matilda that I could have?" asked Willis.

Lisa shrugged off the blanket, tucked it tight around Brandon, then took a picture from the scrapbook she had been working on earlier that evening and handed it to Willis. "That's our Matilda and our son Brandon." Her tears started again.

"That's the boy sitting on the couch?" asked Willis.

"Yes," said Lisa.

"Could I ask him some questions?" asked Willis.

"He seems very upset right now," said Lisa.

"He's been real quiet, Brandon's not usually like that. I think he's been through enough tonight," said Brad. "He needs some R&R from this trauma. Give him a day or so before you talk to him, okay?"

"I'll call tomorrow to see how things are going here and set up a time for the interview," said Willis. "I think I've got everything I need. Anything you two would like to add?"

Brad looked at Lisa, who shook her head. "No, ma'am."

"How about you, Edie?"

"I've got nothing to add," said Edie. "Lisa, Brad,

I'm going to talk with Deputy Willis for a moment before going home, will you be okay here?"

Both nodded.

As Edie and Deputy Willis left the house, they heard Lisa say to Brad, "Edie will find her for us."

Edie made sure the VandenHuevels' house was locked, and then closed the door behind her before joining Deputy Willis at the squad.

"You got your work cut out for yourself, Edie."

"Seems as if I've grown a halo since I moved to this town. Can't you see it?"

"I get the same reaction in my neighborhood. Seriously, what are you thinking? Two cousins missing at the same time, are the cases connected?"

"Could be. I don't know. I don't want to dismiss any ideas yet. Don't know which way the facts will lead us. But I don't like two girls missing from the same family and same home. I would sure like to interview Sage Staley's family myself."

"What for? Are you thinking foul play's involved?"

"Not jumping to conclusions, but it is one of the possibilities...among others."

"I hate working cases involving kids," said Willis.

"I do too, Hannah, since I've become a mother. Cases like this have taken on a new urgency for me. But these cases are part of the job we signed on to do, can't push them off on someone else. I'll call you if the family thinks of anything new."

"Thanks," said Willis.

Edie watched Willis drive away, and then turned her attention to the bats as they did aerial acrobatics chasing the night insects that were gathered under the corner street lamp. She took a deep breath. A scent of wood burning, somewhere in the neighborhood. Edie imagined people had sat around a fire roasting marshmallows, making s'mores, and drinking beer or wine, talking, having a good time. The thought was relaxing. "Bonfires, what a great idea."

Chapter 26

†

Morning still came and the sunshine did its job. It woke up Edie. The alarm clock showed it was nine already. Edie pushed herself out of bed, time to face another damned day.

On the way to the kitchen, Phil stopped her with a kiss. "Took your lemon raspberry bread down to the VandenHuevels. Glad you suggested it, they got plenty of casseroles, their fridge can't hold anymore. That poor family looks like zombies; at least they'll have plenty of food to see them through."

"Who'd you tell that Matilda is missing?"

"Sera."

"Wonder who she called."

"Why?"

"I've wondered how the town's gossip tree works, who calls whom, and how the Vanden-Huevels got all the food so quickly."

"Does it matter?"

"No. I'm only curious."

"You look wiped out; I'll keep Hillary with me today."

"What are you planning to do?"

"Detailing my new truck."

"Isn't that a fancy way of saying you're going to clean it?"

"Deeper than cleaning, we're going to make it smell and shine like new."

"How about detailing my car?"

"I think you need a professional to do that."

"Make sure you take plenty of clothes for Hillary."

"Way ahead of you, they're in the diaper bag. Give your daughter a kiss," said Phil, handing Hillary to Edie. "I put some pancakes in the fridge for you."

Edie gave Hillary a kiss and a big bear hug, handed her back to Phil, then waved them goodbye and decided on a run before her breakfast.

During her run, Edie concentrated on putting one foot in front of the other. She needed to keep going; her body was demanding the exercise, and she wanted to forget about Troutbeck. The run wasn't working its usual magic. The ever-increasing problems of Troutbeck and Phil were still front and center in her thoughts. She tried punching the air like Rocky, that didn't help either. She cut her run short and headed back home. It was then she saw a TV news van parked in front of the church before the occupants saw her. She looked around for an escape route. The cornfield next to the road was the only shelter; she stepped down to it, walked a few rows into the field, and then watched for the van to leave.

Out of the van stepped Leigh Stone. "Damn, I thought she was done reporting here." Edie kept her voice low, even though only the cornstalks could hear. She moved to the end of the cornfield nearest the Troutbeck church; she wanted to hear what was being said. She saw Harold Acker walk out of the church's shadow and straight into the clutches of Leigh Stone.

"Excuse me, sir, I'm Leigh Stone, TV reporter, may I ask you a few questions?"

"Yes," said Harold, looking her up and down.

Don't do it, Harold, it's a trap, Edie wanted to shout. Then she wondered if maybe he saw this as his fifteen minutes of fame.

"We'll be recording our conversation, and it may be on the news this evening. Is that okay?"

"Stop yapping, and start talking, girlie."

Now, that's the Harold I know, thought Edie.

"Before we start, I need to know a few

basics," Leigh Stone informed Harold, flashing a smile at him.

"Them smiles don't work on me, girlie. Got used to them smiles being flashed when I worked down at that nudie place and watched them naked girls con drunk men out of their money. The only smile that done me in was my Mamie's. What do you need to know?"

"A few basics; to begin, what is your name?"

"Harold Acker."

"How long have you lived in this town?"

"Since before I was born."

"The other questions will be asked when we begin filming. Is that okay?"

"Get going, girlie. My breakfast is waiting."

Leigh Stone straightened her clothes, seemed to stand a little taller, and cued her cameraman before talking. "It is early morning in sleepy little Troutbeck, often described as a backwater of Dane County."

"No it ain't, it's a speed trap. Keeps the sheriff and this church rolling in money," said Harold.

Leigh Stone ignored him and continued. "This is a place where neighbors watch out for each other and their doors are seldom locked."

"They will be now, girlie," Harold pointed out.

"And now two girls from this sleepy little village have suddenly gone missing. This is Harold

Acker, a longtime resident of Troutbeck. Harold, what can you tell us about the missing girls?"

"They're missing."

"What can you tell us about the girls themselves?"

"Two of the sweetest girls on the face of the earth, excepting my Mamie Robin, but she isn't with us no more."

"I'm sorry to hear that. Do you know what the police are doing to find the girls?"

"We've got the best damn cops working to find those girls. I'm done talking to you. I've had my morning talk with my Mamie, now I want my breakfast." Harold continued his interrupted walk home.

"Well, that was a useless interview." Leigh Stone's mouth closed, then tightened; she held the mike up in the air like a hammer.

"Temper. You're leaving soon, you can stand us for a few more days," said the cameraman.

"Let's wrap this up, that old fool didn't know anything. Where the fuck is she? I was told she always takes a morning run."

"Were you trying to ambush someone?" asked the cameraman.

"Mind your own fucking business," said Leigh Stone.

"You've got an open mike," the cameraman reminded her. "Where did you learn your ethics? I've told you before, I don't do gotcha stories."

"I'm done with this two-bit town and this flyover country anyway." Leigh Stone stomped her foot, handed the mike to the cameraman, and got into the van.

When Edie saw the cameraman climb into the van, she came out of her hiding place, stepped into the middle of the road, and waved goodbye.

Chapter 27

†

The pancakes Phil had left for her and the instant coffee she made weren't what Edie wanted; she poured a bowl of cereal and made a pot of coffee, taking them over to the rocking chair. She set the bowl and coffee on the cold wood stove, sat in the rocking chair, put her feet on the stove, and stared out the window. Nothing but cornfields, hayfields, and soybean fields as far as the eye could see, until they bumped up against the dense stand of oaks, hickories, and box elders in Breitenbach's woods. What a pleasure to let her thoughts wander and settle on nothing, no Phil, no Hillary, no nobody to interrupt her. The rest of the day belonged to her. What a relief from the past week, when she had patrolled the edge of the abyss in Madison. Now she wanted to enjoy the boredom of nothingness. But Sage...and Matilda...and Yesenia crept into her consciousness. The week had come full circle. It started with Sage and seemed to be ending with Sage and Matilda.

She watched as two bicyclists came into view. "Damn, that's Brandon. Why is he out biking? Should he be out biking?" She'd walk down to the VandenHuevels later and find out why. There was a knock at the front door. Edie did nothing. If she ignored it, maybe they would go away. There was another knock. She pushed herself out of the chair and went to see who was being so rude to disturb her on one of her few days off. On the way to answer the door, she considered bawling out whoever was at her front door; she quickly rejected it. She had another forty, maybe fifty years before she could become one of the crazy old coots of Troutbeck.

It was Brandon and another kid. Damn, she'd be adding to Brandon's stress if she yelled at him. Instead, she greeted him as if it were a typical day. "Morning, Brandon, good to see you out and about."

"Thanks, Mrs. Best."

Edie's six-second delay kicked in; if Brandon's parents and Matilda hadn't clued him in, she wasn't going to. "What can I do for you, Brandon?"

"My mom said I should come and talk to you. Me and Tim stopped in hours ago, but Mr. Best said you were sleeping and to come back later. So here we are. What do you want to ask us?"

"Come on in, we'll talk in the family area."

Brandon and Tim followed Edie to the back room. She stopped in the kitchen long enough to put some snickerdoodles on a plate and fill glasses of water for the boys that she then placed on the counter in front of them.

While they munched, she began the interview. "What have you two been doing?"

"Biking," said Brandon.

"Did you talk to Deputy Willis this morning?"

"No, my dad said I didn't have to talk to no one for a while. Except you. He said that I should get outside and do nothing. That's when Tim and I decided to go biking."

"I'm wondering what you can tell me about your sister."

"Geez, Mrs. Best, you see her as much as I do. She's a girl, and girls are weird."

A few more years and he might not get enough of them, thought Edie. "That's not completely true, Brandon. Tell me, when did you last see Matilda?"

"The day she went to stay with her friend," said Brandon, the words running together.

That was an awfully fast reply. Had he been thinking about it for a while? "When was that?"

"A few days ago. How am I supposed to remember? It's summer, I don't gotta remember nothing until school starts. Can we go now? We want to break our speed record for making it around the block."

"Sure. Brandon, before you two go, are you going to introduce me to your friend?" said Edie.

"Didn't you hear me? I already called him Tim. Okay, okay, don't look at me that way; you look like my mother right now. Mrs. Best, this is my friend."

Edie didn't push the etiquette lesson further.

Brandon and Tim grabbed the rest of the cookies and stuffed them in their pockets, heading for the front door. Not hearing the door close, Edie followed them. It was open. Before closing the door, she watched the boys jump on their bikes and glide to Brandon's house. She wondered what their fastest time around the block was. Must be really slow if they can talk to me, eat some cookies, and still beat it. But kids will be kids and exploring is what they do, at least that's how she remembered those years. She closed the door.

Edie went back to her rocking chair. The cereal was soggy, the coffee cold; she put them back on the wood stove, she'd dump them later. She rocked and thought about Brandon. She hadn't had many encounters with him. She knew of his character and quirks from Matilda's reports. But still, something about him wasn't adding up. There was a disconnect somewhere that she wasn't getting. Another damned disconnect in that family, what was wrong? He had said nothing during the wee hours of the morning, just sat and huddled next to his mother. Was this a typical brotherly response? She couldn't tell, she didn't ever have one. This afternoon he didn't look scared or upset that Matilda was missing. Was this the way he dealt with his sister and cousin, who had gone missing in the same week? Or did he hate Matilda and was glad to be rid of her? No, to her Matilda and Brandon always looked as if they liked each other. The more Edie thought, the wilder the scenarios became. Edie decided that this was a problem to put on the back burner and let simmer for a while.

When Edie finally pushed herself out of the rocker she noticed a touch of yellow in the soybean fields—summer was fading fast. That thought surprised her; the rhythms of farm life were creeping into hers. She needed to enjoy the last days of summer before the autumn rains came. Remembrance of last night's burning wood scent triggered the urge to have a bonfire of her own.

Edie invited her Troutbeck friends to the bonfire.

Sera Voss was the first to say yes. Edie didn't stop at the VandenHuevels; she saw that every curtain in every room was closed. She hesitated at Grizzly Jack's, and then decided that it would be best if Grizzly met Troutbeck residents on her own, one at a time. Bridget said she wouldn't miss the bonfire. Carole insisted on bringing Ray's new brew.

On the way home, Edie reconsidered inviting Grizzly Jack to the bonfire. She stopped at the corner store and knocked.

"Girlie, you found the culprit yet?" Grizzly Jack asked before could Edie could speak.

"My name is Edie Swift."

"I know your name, what I don't know is if you've found him."

"Who?"

"The squatter."

"Haven't started..."

"Nothing swift about you, what are you waiting for?"

"For it not to be my day off."

"Can you talk English?"

"It's my day off; I've got other things to do."

"Since when do cops take a day off?"

In this town, never, thought Edie. She counted to six, then ten, and then thought it was best that the first encounter between Grizzly Jack and Troutbeck should be in a group, there was strength in numbers. "I'm having a bonfire tonight at my place, how about coming?"

"Is that an invitation?"

"Yes."

"When and where?"

"My place, last house at the edge of the world. Dusk."

"Don't need any directions, it won't take a genius to figure out—I'll see the fire and smell the smoke. Don't know if I can make it, I'm still unpacking," said Grizzly and shut the door.

"At least I did the right thing," said Edie, walking home. "How do I love thee, Phil Best, let me count the ways: I live in Troutbeck. I'm drinking Ray's beer. I've invited the newest town scrooge to a party. I usually shut my mouth around your mother. I've solved two murders here. I live here—I've said that, but that one counts for a lot. By my calculations, you owe me big time, mister." And when the opportunity presented itself, she would tell him exactly what he owed her, big time.

Chapter 28

†

The house was clean, and Hillary and Phil were gone for the rest of the day. It was the perfect time to catch up on her sleep. Edie lay on her bed, but sleep wouldn't come. She picked up her library book—that didn't put her to sleep. She went to the kitchen, turned on the computer—a game of Solitaire and then FreeCell didn't make her sleepy. Thoughts of Yesenia popped into her head. The phrase, once a cop, always a cop, ran through her head. She gave up, she might as well work.

Aunt Jill was making lunch for the farm crew when Edie knocked. Aunt Jill opened the door for her. "Sweetie, you don't have to knock. Just give a holler when you come in. I like to know who is in my house."

"I'm not a Troutbeckian, yet. And I'd like to keep it that way."

"What does that mean?"

"Troutbeck residents are used to walking into anyone's house unasked and unannounced."

"But, Edie, my house is your house. Consider that your neighbors have a long history together. Some of them may even be related...or maybe all of them."

"This is your house? You're moving in with Hank?"

"You know what I mean. You also know that I've been living in sin with Hank for a while now."

"When did you start using the phrase living in sin?"

"Excuse me, I don't know why that popped out of my mouth, must have been channeling my mother. Are you here for lunch?"

"I didn't come to eat. I'm here to talk to Yesenia."

"She usually eats with the rest of the crew. Why not join us? The food is almost ready."

"Okay. Eating lunch with Yesenia might make it easier for her to talk to me. Can you arrange for us to eat in private, away from prying eyes and ears?"

Aunt Jill considered her niece's request for a moment. "I'll serve the food out on the picnic tables. You and Yesenia can eat in here."

"I'd like you to be with us when I talk to Yesenia."

"That's a good idea. Yessie might be more comfortable with me at the table. The three of us can eat and talk in here, and Hank can serve the food to the rest of the crew. He may be out of practice, but he's intelligent—he can figure out how to do it."

Edie put the food and plates on the tables that she and Aunt Jill placed under the trees. Aunt Jill called the crew to eat and instructed Hank on what to do. When Yesenia got in line, Aunt Jill took her hand and led her into the kitchen. "Yessie, we girls are going to eat in the kitchen." She guided Yesenia to the kitchen table, put a plate filled with food in front of her, then she and Edie sat down on either side of her. Yesenia moved her chair a few inches closer to Aunt Jill.

They were almost done eating when Edie looked at Aunt Jill and gave a quick nod.

"Yessie. Edie would like to talk with you."

Yessie dropped her fork on the plate, folded her hands in her lap, then looked from Aunt Jill to Edie and back again, then looked back down at her hands.

"Yessie, tell me about the white car, again. Please."

Silence.

"Yessie, what did the man in the white car look like?"

Silence.

Aunt Jill put an arm around Yessie's shoulders. "Yessie, you need to talk to someone. Edie wants to help you. She is my niece and I trust her."

"No, ella es policía, me meterá en la cárcel y me deportarán. Mis hermanos y mis primos sabrán que pasó conmigo. Esta es mi tierra ahora, no quiero que me saquen de aquí." Yesenia spoke to her hands. The words poured out as if a floodgate had been opened. "Mi madre me dijo que no había nada que hacer en nuestro pueblo más que tener chiquillos. Me dijo que tendría una mejor vida en el norte, que siguiera a mis hermanos, que la vida sería más fácil aquí. Pero que consigo? Mucho trabajo duro, nada más. No puedo salir sin que alguien me escupa o me llame puta mexicana o me gritan, acusándome de quitarles sus trabajos. Los gringos limpian mierda de vaca? No. Y los gringos ordeñan vacas dos o tres veces al día? No. Ellos se comen el queso y la nieve se beben la leche que con tanto trabajo ayudo a producir. No hay nadie aquí que me defienda? Alguien en quién confiar? Cómo puedo vivir aquí? Cómo puedo encontrar a personas que me apoyen o que estén conmigo por el resto de mi vida? No hay nadie aquí para mi. Esto no se supone que fuera asi, se suponía que fuera más sencillo." And the tears followed the stream of anger.

Aunt Jill looked stunned at Yesenia's outpouring

of grief and anger. Yesenia's tears turned to sobs. Aunt Jill wrapped her arms around the young girl.

Edie waited for an opening. She had seen this before. Quietly, calmly, she asked again, "Yessie, dime sobre el carro blanco."

"No puedo," whispered Yessie.

"Porqué no?" asked Edie.

"Porque entonces recordaré."

"Recordarás que?"

Silence.

Edie tried another tack. "Me contaste que recogías flores en el bosque. Fuiste allí esa mañana?"

"Sí."

"Hacía sol esa mañana?"

"No, había nubes."

"Fuiste al bosque antes o después de ordeñar?"

"Ya había terminado con mi trabajo, siempre termino con mis tareas."

"Entonces... fuiste a recoger flores?"

"Soy una chica. No me gusta apestar a vaca todo el día."

"Fuiste al bosque por flores?"

"Sí."

"Sabes los nombres de las flores?"

"No, nunca vi esas flores en mi pueblo."

"De qué color eran las flores?"

"Algunas blancas, otras moradas, algunas amarillas."

"Pasó algún carro?"

215

"No, sólo el blanco. Paró, se fue, y luego volvió y paró por mucho tiempo." Tears flooded down Yesenia's face.

"Hablaste con el hombre que manejaba el carro?"

"No, escuché la puerta abrirse y después cerrarse. Entonces me agarró, me apretó el cuello, y bajó mis pantalones...." Yessie's sobs shook her body.

Aunt Jill pulled Yesenia closer into her sheltering arms. "Edie, did you understand any of what Yessie said?"

"Every word."

"It was all one word to me, but I got the gist of it."

"Aunt Jill, when did you learn Spanish?"

"Picked it up since I've been coming to the farm, had to, wanted to talk with people here, and I'm not dumb enough to think that we stand apart from the world. Where'd you learn yours? I know you, Spanish wasn't the language you took in high school or college."

"Learned some on the job, part of my responsibility to talk with and help all people, and the rest I learned at Madison Area Technical College—sorry, forgot that it's now Madison College. What are you going to do with Yessie?"

"Keep her with me."

"Good."

Chapter 29

†

Edie placed a bucket of water a few feet from the fire pit and was building the fire when Sera arrived with lawn chairs. "How many are coming, Edie?"

"You, me, Bridget, Carole, maybe Grizzly Jack, a real girls' night out."

"Who's Grizzly Jack?"

"You haven't met her? I am floored that I know something the rest of the town doesn't. She's our newest neighbor, the proud owner of what was the corner store."

"Is Lisa coming?"

"No, last time I walked past their house, it was buttoned up tight."

"Poor kids. She should come, they need to be out among friends."

"They sure do, but you'll never convince Lisa of that."

"I'll stop over tomorrow with muffins and have a talk with her. Do you want some? I made plenty, raspberry ones. Got a good crop this year. I'll go get you some of those muffins and a bowl of raspberries."

Edie put another log on the fire, set up a table, then placed chairs around the fire pit, got another folding table from the garage—she didn't know how much food and beer her neighbors would bring.

Sera came back with her raspberries and muffins. Carole was right behind her pulling a cooler filled with beer and a bottle or two of root beer for Bridget. And Bridget brought up the rear with chips and dip.

As the women settled into the chairs and opened the first round of beer, Grizzly Jack showed up lugging a hug bag.

Edie stood up. "Glad you could make it, Ms. Jack."

"We're neighbors, you can call me Grizzly."

"Okay, Grizzly, let me introduce you to some of your other neighbors. Everyone, this is Grizzly Jack, you all know where she lives. Grizzly, Sera Voss is the one with the salt-and-pepper hair. She lives right next door to me. On the other side of Sera is Bridget Briggs, also known as the owner of the Halloween house—she lives in the village, across the road and down a few houses from you. And next to her is Carole Rhyme, she lives one street back of Bridget—she knows everything."

"Nice to meet you Grizzly," said Carole. "Grab a beer from the cooler and have a seat. You're in luck tonight; this is one of Ray's better brews."

"Who's Ray?" Grizzly asked, taking empanadas, fruit tartlets, and a cheese plate with dates and nuts from her bag and setting them on a table. She grabbed a beer and joined the women at the fire.

"My husband," replied Carole.

"He makes some fine beer," said Bridget.

"Don't pay any attention to her, she doesn't know her beers," said Edie. "Half a glass of beer and she's under the table. Right now she's guzzling root beer."

"One of the finest I've ever drank," replied Bridget.

"His brews haven't killed me yet. Interesting name you have, Ms. Jack," said Carole.

"Got it in first grade, but it really started with my parents," said Grizzly.

"Mine too," said Sera. "My parents stuck me with Seraphina when all the other girls were Judy, Debbie, Nancy, Linda, Dianne. But I got Seraphina."

"If that's all you got to complain about, you're lucky," Grizzly Jack pointed out.

"But I always wanted to be a Linda or a Sue, like the other girls."

"Sera doesn't sound too bad a name to me, suck it up and let it go. By the looks of your hair, you should've done that a long time ago," said Grizzly.

219

"I got Grizel. Where my parents got it, I don't know. The boys in my first-grade class changed it to Grizzly; I've been called that ever since."

"Sorry about that," said Bridget. "But kids do grow out of meanness, you know."

"Do they?" asked Grizzly. "In my experience, they rarely grow out of it."

"Most do. Most young people act out to impress their peers. It usually doesn't mean anything," said Bridget.

"I don't agree with that; words matter as much as action. How do you know so much about kids?" asked Grizzly.

"I see them one hundred and eighty days a year, not including summer school. I'm the high school principal," said Bridget.

"My condolences," said Grizzly.

"I like my job," said Bridget.

"Most of the time," said Carole.

"And what do you do?" Grizzly asked Carole.

"Drink Ray's brews and cut hair."

"At the same time?" asked Grizzly

Edie choked on her beer. "Depends on how angry she is; usually she's a good stylist—unless you make her mad."

"Unless you don't pay your tab," Carole corrected her.

"What you grousing about? I'm caught up," said Edie.

The women eased into banter about the sunset, the star-filled night, the miserable August weather, local news, and politics.

Edie leaned back in her chair to stare at the stars' light display. She could now pick out a few constellations and satellites. "I wish Matilda were here, she could tell me what I'm seeing."

"Who's Matilda?" asked Grizzly.

"A girl from the village, she's missing," said Bridget.

"So's her cousin," said Carole.

"Why'd they leave, too quiet here?" asked Grizzly.

No one answered.

Don't let this town fool you, it isn't as peaceful as it looks, Edie wanted to say.

"Cops working on it?" Grizzly asked.

"Yes. And I haven't heard anything about the case yet," said Edie, trying to head off the next questions she knew would be asked. Those questions came anyway.

"And what are you finding?" asked Carole.

"She won't tell me," said Phil, pulling a beer from the cooler. "She claims that if I don't know, I won't have to lie, if I'm ever put on the witness stand or quizzed by my neighbors."

"Didn't hear you come out, Phil. Grizzly, this is Phil Best. Phil, meet our newest neighbor, Grizzly Jack."

"You two married?" asked Grizzly.

"No," Sera, Carole, and Bridget said in unison.

"Good for you," said Grizzly.

"How about you, are you married?" Carole asked.

"Moved here because if you blink while driving through, you miss the town. Didn't come for its nosy neighbors," Grizzly replied. "Tell me, when was the last time you beat your kids?"

Edie, Carole, and Bridget looked at each other with raised eyebrows, Edie's description of Grizzly as one more crotchety old person was dead on.

"Last time they were in town and did something wrong," Carole answered, not missing a beat.

Phil shrugged his shoulders. He turned to the food on the table, popped a few raspberries, then picked up a folded pastry. "These are good. What are they called?"

"Empanadas," said Grizzly. "A South American food."

"Where did you get them?" Phil asked, before he stuffed another one in his mouth.

"I made them," said Grizzly.

The women rushed to join Phil at the table. Phil picked up another empanada and moved on to the tartlets. "Delicious. You made these, too?"

"Yes," said Grizzly.

"Are you a cook?" asked Sera.

"Among other things," replied Grizzly. "Try the cheese; put the dates and nuts on top."

"What do you do?" asked Bridget, following Phil to the tartlets.

"Name says it all, Grizzly Jack—Jack-of-all-trades."

The women and Phil stuffed themselves, then grabbed a favorite beer before settling in to watch the fire die.

Well before midnight, Edie and Phil were left alone to watch the embers shatter into ashes.

Edie watched as Phil stood up and stretched; soon she knew that he too would leave and she would be left to extinguish the fire. This wasn't like the old days when everyone hung around to greet the dawn.

"I'm calling it quits, got a long day tomorrow. Coming?" said Phil.

"No. Looks like I'm the sole keeper of the flame tonight," replied Edie.

"You're not going to put more wood on the fire, are you?"

"No, just want to linger here for a moment before I pour water on it."

Phil left.

Edie leaned back to view the stars, what a marvel to behold.

The fire had burned down to mostly ashes

when Edie dumped a pail of water on it, stirred it around, and stepped back to watch as the steam spiraled into the night sky. She folded the chairs, carried them to the garage, and leaned them against the doorjamb as she searched for the light switch. She flipped on the garage light. Directly below it was the trash bag Grizzly Jack had given her. Maybe a cop's work was never done; now seemed the right time to open the bag. She ripped open the plastic bag, emptied it on the floor, and crouched down to examine its contents. Fast food wrappers, freeze-dried hiking meals, munchies, empty yogurt containers, diet pop cans. Edie relaxed, the dots of one case were beginning to connect and lead to another. She stacked the chairs inside and closed the garage door to protect the evidence from all the nocturnal animals. She went back to the fire for one last look and one more poking around it to make sure there were no embers, and then scouted the area for anything that might have been forgotten. At the edge of her lawn, she glanced over at Breitenbach's woods; a faint smoke trail rose above them. She smiled. Tomorrow would be soon enough to investigate its origins.

Chapter 30

†

Edie was dressed before Phil opened his eyes.

"Where you going?" Phil asked.

"Out."

"I can see that, give me the details," said Phil.

"Going for a long walk, don't know when I'll be back."

"What am I supposed to do with Hillary?"

"Watch her."

"I've got deliveries to make; I've got to catch up on Max's route. My customers are screaming at me."

"Don't worry; I'll be back before you leave."

"Again, give me details. Specifics."

"Can't give you what I don't have. Right now, all I have are hunches."

"So this is a wild-goose chase you're going on."

"Something like that, but a little more concrete, maybe."

"Damn it, Edie, I'm thinking that I should listen to my mother's warnings about you."

"Maybe you should listen to her. See you later." Edie pulled on a light jacket, stuffed the flashlight she kept on the bedside table into a pocket, her phone into the other.

Phil followed her into the kitchen, where Edie stuffed a couple of Grizzly Jack's tarts into a bag. "I thought those were for me," Phil complained.

"Nope. Using these to distract any bears I might run into, heard there were some in the area."

Edie parked her car north of Breitenbach's woods and waited. She had put in a request for Deputy Johnson and Detective Fitzgerald to meet her there. It was Deputy Hannah Willis who pulled up in a squad car.

"Hey, Edie, got a call that you wanted someone out here. What's going on?" asked Willis

"I'm checking out a hunch, wanted backup if I'm right. I asked for Johnson or Fitzgerald, where are they?"

"No clue. Why?"

"Told them I'd keep them updated on what's happening with their cases. This hike might help both of them."

"So, what's happening?"

"We're going for a walk in the woods," said Edie.

"Bring a jacket, you may need it for protection, I don't know what type of brush we'll find in there."

"This isn't one of those snipe hunts new recruits are sent on, is it?" asked Willis, getting a jacket from the trunk. "I've already been on one those. Anything else we might need, before I lock up the car?"

"I got a Hodag hunt on my first time out. I don't think you'll need anything else, I hope. Follow me." Edie crossed the road and headed into the woods.

Edie was a couple hundred feet into the woods when Willis caught up with her. "Could you slow down a bit? I'm not used to being in the wild," Willis said, pushing a tree branch out of her way.

"Quieter, please. I don't want to startle any bears or other creatures that might be here."

Willis let go of the branch, it whacked her in the face. "Bears! I didn't know bears were in this part of Wisconsin." She held the branch away from her and ran her other hand over her face, checking for any bleeding.

"Neither did I until recently. Let me tell you what I've been reading about black bears. They're in Dane County and the surrounding counties. No one knows whether they are resident bears, just passing through, or ones that are looking for a new home. Another thing I've read, we're supposed to make noise to let them know we're around. But don't do that now. I want you to stay close to me and quiet."

"No problem there, you can count on me to do both. But I'm giving you notice that if I see a bear, I'm screaming and probably running the other way. What are we looking for?"

"The source of the smoke I saw last night."

"Shouldn't we call the fire department?"

"No. I think it is a fire built by Matilda VandenHuevel."

"The girl we're looking for? How did you jump from smoke to Matilda?" asked Willis, stepping on Edie's heels.

"Careful, you don't have to ride my butt. When I saw the smoke coming from here last night, everything fell into place. Before then there was something that wasn't connecting in what I was seeing and hearing about Matilda."

"Like what?"

"Matilda was supposed to be at a friend's house for a few days. Turned out it was an old teenage trick. A series of misdirection: you tell your parents you'll be at so and so's house, they tell their parents they'll be at another friend's house, it goes on until one, maybe none, of the parents understand that they've been conned."

"Never did that," said Deputy Willis.

"It's an elaborate setup. Takes brainpower to keep the stories straight," said Edie.

"Are you speaking from experience?"

"Taking the fifth on this one."

"What else fell into place for you?"

"Well, then there's her brother, never seemed upset that Matilda was missing except that one night, but he could have been mirroring his parents' emotions. Next, Grizzly Jack, that's the name of my new neighbor, moves into the unoccupied corner store in Troutbeck and finds that a vagrant was sleeping in her place...or maybe it was Goldilocks. Then last night I saw the smoke spiraling out of the woods."

"Coincidences. How do they add up to Matilda?"

Edie stopped. Willis bumped into her.

"We have to slow down and keep our eyes open for signs of activity."

"Like what?"

"A dead campfire. Paths. Latrines. Matilda probably dug a pit latrine for them to use."

"There's more than one of them?"

"Did I forget to mention Sage is probably with Matilda?"

Willis nodded and whispered, "The cousin?"

"Yes, the other missing girl, Matilda's cousin."

"This could be a Nancy Drew mystery, The Case of the Missing Cousin. Finish connecting the dots for me, Edie."

"Sage is the first one who went missing, her

car was recently found in Madison, and so we are all looking for her there. But then all that other stuff I've mentioned happened. It's all adding up to me thinking that Matilda is helping her cousin hide out."

"Nice theory, but how are you going to prove it? What are they hiding for? Why hide out here? Why wouldn't Matilda be in Madison or someplace far, far away with Sage?"

"Don't know what they're hiding out from. Everything I've observed of Matilda, she likes her family; I don't think Sage likes hers. And we are going to discover all of that by talking with the girls. Now, shhh. Look over to your left, see the fire ring? Start looking for a tent, it can't be too far away."

"I don't see a thing."

"How many cases like this have you been on?"

"This is my first."

"Get used to it. We keep our eyes open and follow the evidence, wherever it leads, even if it leads us into the woods. See it? The tent's about fifteen feet to our right, under those low hanging branches."

"I do now," Willis whispered back.

"You know, if Matilda ever goes over to the dark side, we're in trouble."

Once pointed out, the tent was easy to spot.

"Good, follow me." Edie walked over to the tent. In front of it, the weeds were trampled and the lowest tree branches were either broken or cut off. "Good morning, girls," Edie called out.

There wasn't a sound that came from the tent.

"Matilda, Sage, you're burning daylight," said Edie.

Edie knelt in front of the tent, unzipped it, saw two sleeping bags with something burrowing into each. "Time to rise and shine, girls."

Chapter 31

†

"**G**o away," said Matilda, her voice muffled by the sleeping bag.

"Leave us alone," said Sage. "We haven't done anything."

"Can't, you two are missing juveniles. It is our job to find you and return you to your families. We've found you. Now all we have to do is to return you to your parents."

"I'd like to see you try it. You can't catch us both," said Sage.

"No, I can't, that's why I brought backup. Deputy Hannah Willis, come on over and meet Matilda VandenHuevel and Sage Staley."

Willis walked over and squatted next to Edie in front of the tent.

"Girls, this is Deputy Hannah Willis. Willis, this is Matilda and Sage."

"Girls, we're here to take you back home," said Willis.

"I won't let you take her back," said Matilda, kicking out of her sleeping bag and throwing herself on top of Sage.

"Why not, Matilda?" asked Edie.

The girls did not answer. Matilda knew she had a right not to speak. Sage did what Matilda did.

Edie tried a different tack. "Matilda, Sage, we've got a new neighbor, but I guess you already know that. Anyway, her name is Grizzly Jack, she's a good cook. Got some of the tarts she brought to my bonfire last night," said Edie. "That was an interesting night, talked with a few neighbors, shared some food and drink, we all wondered where Matilda and Sage were. After everyone left I stayed up late to make sure the fire was dead."

"Is that when you saw the smoke?" asked Matilda.

"Not much gets past you, Matilda," said Edie. "Yes, that is when I saw the smoke swirling over these woods. Come on out and try these tarts. They are delicious. Wished I'd saved a couple of Sera's raspberry muffins, maybe she still has a few. Maybe she'll make a new batch for you. She says the raspberries canes are full."

Matilda rolled off the top of Sage's sleeping bag and tried to pull the sleeping bag away from her. "Come on, Sage, we can't hide and we can't run."

"Like hell I can't. They're not going to make me go home," said Sage, grabbing the sleeping bag back. "And don't you leave the tent either. You go out there, we're probably goners. They probably got their guns pointed at us. If they don't arrest us, they'll shoot us. They'll shoot us and leave us here to rot. I've heard about police killing unarmed people."

"Only one way out of that sleeping bag, Sage. Why don't you come out and join us?" Edie coaxed.

"I'm staying here," was Sage's muffled reply.

"Have it your way. It'll get pretty raunchy in there," said Edie.

Matilda looked at Edie and Willis. "Edie wouldn't do that. Come on, Sage, this is Edie you're talking about. We sit for her kid. We watched stars with her. She paid for your haircut. Sage, she's got food. I'm hungry. Brandon didn't bring us enough food yesterday."

Sage crawled out of her sleeping bag. Both girls left the tent, stood up, and stretched. Sage bent down to get her shoes out of the tent.

"Leave them there, Sage," Edie instructed.

"I've got to pee," said Sage. "There's lots of dirt and twigs and stuff between here and the latrine."

"I understand, but you're still walking barefoot to the latrine. Willis will accompany you," said Edie. "Sage, I'm pretty sure that Matilda cleared a path to the latrine she dug. You'll only get mud on your feet."

"See, Matilda, they have us under arrest and are torturing us already," said Sage.

"More like protective custody," said Edie.

"Then why can't I have my shoes?" asked Sage.

"Bare feet will slow down your exit plan," said Edie.

"I'll go with them, I've got to pee, too," said Matilda.

"Matilda, one person at a time," said Edie. "When Deputy Willis comes back with Sage, she'll escort you to the pit. Until then, you can stay with me."

"Sage, hurry up, I don't want to piss myself—I don't have any more clean clothes," Matilda yelled to her. She turned to Edie, "How did you know that I cleared a latrine and made a path to it?"

"Matilda, I've only known you for a short time, but I've seen you think things out and prepare—you don't do things half-assed."

While Willis and Sage went to the latrine, Edie pulled the sleeping bags from the tent, unzipped each, shook them out, and spread them on the ground. Matilda and Edie sat on them and stared at each other. When Deputy Willis and Sage returned, it was Sage's turn to stare at Edie while Willis escorted Matilda to the latrine. When Matilda and Willis were back, Edie opened the bag of tarts.

"Hand sanitizer first, Sage," Matilda reminded her cousin. Matilda crawled into the tent, took a bottle from the first aid kit, squirted some into her hand, and then into Sage's.

When they were finished rubbing their hands, Edie offered the tarts to the girls—it looked as if the girls inhaled the goodies.

"Well, girls, where should we start this conversation?" asked Edie.

"How about you explaining how you found us?" said Sage.

"I connected the dots when I saw the smoke above these woods," said Edie.

"What were the dots?" blurted Matilda.

"Not in any particular order: your brother didn't seem overly concerned about your disappearance, our new neighbor had evidence that someone was sleeping in her house, the smoke from the woods, and you, Matilda, you like your family too much to run away," said Edie. "I did my part, now it's your turn. Why come here?"

"Sage stayed in the old corner store for a few days because it was empty and close by, but it had been sold and I didn't know when the new owner would move in, so I got things ready for us to come here. It was the only thing that I could think of," said Matilda.

"Nice job with your camp," said Willis.

"Thanks," replied Matilda.

"How long were you planning on being out here?" asked Edie.

"Until they forgot about me," said Sage.

Edie considered the girl's statement. "Sage, you are unforgettable. But who is this they?"

"My parents," said Sage.

"That won't happen," said Edie. "Right now, I'm told, they are very upset."

"They're pretending. They're good liars. He's never going to touch me again—ever," Sage shouted at the sleeping bag, avoiding all eye contact.

Matilda wrapped a trembling Sage in a bear hug.

When Sage's anger stopped echoing through the woods, Edie spoke, softly. "Who is this 'he' you are talking about?"

There was no answer.

"Tell me about it," Edie whispered.

"I was in 'their' house, alone. He came home, grabbed me by my hair, then dragged me into my bedroom, shoved me on my bed, then...then..." Sage couldn't finish, she was bawling. Between the sobs, the rest of the story came out. One word, with long pauses between each, at a time. And the story ended with, "Daddys aren't supposed to do that."

Edie and Willis stared at each other. They could piece together the rest of the story, and they had heard similar stories, way too many stories like Sage's. But they also knew that soon Sage would need to say the words that would make the incest concrete to the rest of the world, and start the justice system toward making Sage whole again, if that could ever be achieved. And somehow that system might get Sage the help she would need to handle a lifetime of unexpected flashbacks.

Edie moved next to Sage, dropped her arms over Matilda's bear hug and held her. It didn't take long for Edie's shirt to be soaked with tears. She held Sage until her rage subsided. "Sage, I'm sorry, but we need to take you and Matilda back with us."

"We'll just run away again," said Matilda.

"Then I will find you. Again. Think, Matilda, Sage needs more than running away right now," said Edie, looking at her over Sage's head.

"Like what?" demanded Matilda.

"Someone to help her get through this injustice, this assault, and her rage. She needs someone to help find solid emotional ground so she can live the rest of her life."

"No one's helped her before," said Matilda. Then she whispered, "Excepting maybe you, Edie."

"And you, Matilda. Sage may never have said anything to anyone before she told you. Maybe she never found the right person to help her. Then she told you and you did something about it. Matilda, we need to give other people the chance to help Sage," said Edie.

"And if they don't?" demanded Matilda.

"Then we will search for someone who will," said Edie. "But first we need to take the both of you back with us. You are missing juveniles. We found you two; we need to take you back."

Deputy Willis stepped in. "Matilda, we'll go back to your house, I'll update my sergeant on this case, and then call Children's Services and tell them about you."

"You promise, Edie? You gotta promise to help us," said Matilda.

"I'll keep my eye on her," Edie promised.

Matilda thought for a bit. "I trust her, Sage. How about you?"

"I'm okay with her, if you're okay with her," said Sage.

Matilda made the decision. "Let's go back, Sage."

Edie typed her initial report on Deputy Willis's MDT while Willis called her sergeant, then the Dane County Department of Human Services. When she got home, Phil was in an explosive mood.

"Where the hell have you been?" Phil screamed when Edie walked in the door.

Edie dropped into a defensive mode, assumed an athletic stance, feet spread hip-length apart, shoulders down and back; it was an automatic response. "Digging myself deeper into Troutbeck's gratitude by solving two of their problems."

Phil took a step back. "When is it my turn? When are you going to solve my problems?"

"It seems only moments ago you were telling me that I was the superhero of Troutbeck, and that I should get used to it. And, this is a big one, Phil, I wasn't supposed to solve your problems. Either I'm always on call as a cop when I'm at home or I shut the door on this little town. Suck it up, buttercup; you can't have it both ways."

"But I needed you here today."

"I was doing my job. I found Matilda and Sage. I'm here now. What do you need?"

"You to watch your daughter."

"Hillary has two parents. It's your job to be with her when I can't."

"What about my job?" said Phil.

"Parenting is your job, too. And why am I supposed to put my job on hold and you aren't?"

"I should've listened to my mother," yelled Phil, slamming the door behind him as he stormed out of the house.

Edie opened it. "It's not too late," she shouted, slamming the door shut. She counted to ten and opened the door again. "Where are you going?"

"To pick up the slack at work. Someone's gotta make Max's delivery. That someone is me." Phil jumped into his pickup truck and floored it out of the driveway.

"Pick up some grown-up attitudes while you're at it," Edie yelled, slamming the door again.

From the bedroom, Hillary's cries became audible. Edie picked her out of her crib and held her close. "Don't cry, little one, it's only adults being stupid."

Chapter 32

✝

Edie woke to the sound of a soft thud. It wasn't her this time. She picked the book off the floor. That book looked like a keeper, something that would be guaranteed to put her to sleep when nothing else could. Her cell showed 9:15 p.m. She rolled off the couch and walked through the house. Hillary was asleep. All the doors were locked. All the windows were closed and locked. Phil wasn't in their bed. His pickup wasn't in the drive. She considered turning the lamp in the living room off but didn't—Phil would need it when he came home, he didn't like walking into a dark house.

She looked at her cell, 9:35 p.m. Damn. She went to the kitchen, fixed herself a cup of mint tea. And waited.

It was 9:50 p.m., there was no second-guessing or arguing with a cell phone about the correct time.

Edie began to wonder about Phil's absence. Was he having mechanical problems with the new truck? Did he really know the delivery route? Was he gabbing, as usual, with a customer?

At 10:30 p.m., Edie called Phil—someone had to be the adult. It went to his voice mail. Either he's still angry or left his phone in the truck while unloading the truck at a customer's place, she thought. Whatever his reason for not answering his phone, she was stuck in adulthood by herself.

At 11:30 p.m., Edie started to get worried. She checked on Hillary, she was asleep. For a brief moment, Edie considered pulling a chair next to the crib and watching her baby sleep. She didn't, she had learned to let the child sleep. She needed something to do. Edie changed into jeans and T-shirt, and pulled on a sweatshirt. She then went next door to Sera Voss'. It took a couple of knocks on the door to wake Sera.

"Is that you, Phil?" asked Sera from behind her locked front door.

"No, it's me, Edie."

Sera opened the door. "What's wrong?"

"Phil's not home. I need someone to watch Hillary while I go to the shop to check on him."

"Be with you in a minute, I need to change and grab a key for my house."

When they were back at Edie's house, Edie gave Sera instructions. "Make yourself at home; you probably know where everything is. I shouldn't be gone long. You've got my cell number."

Edie drove to Phil's shop. The place was dark. The outdoor security lights turned on when she was at the door punching the code into the keypad to open the shop. The indoor lights came on when she opened the door. Good to know that he had installed some security devices. Phil's pickup was there, but no Phil. She pulled out her cell and tried him again. No answer. She walked into the office, looked through the drivers' routes. She couldn't find a paper trail as to what delivery route Phil was driving that night. She stared at the computer. Phil probably had time to put a tracking unit on the new truck. While the computer was booting up, she searched the desk for the password—she found it stuck on the back of the computer. It took some time to find the tracking program. The new truck did have a tracking unit attached to it—that man was so predictable. It looked like every truck was accounted for and their locations seemed to be legitimate. But nothing was moving. Edie looked again. Why was nothing moving when one of them should be? Why wasn't Phil's new truck moving? Why was it in the Deansville Marsh and not moving?

Edie noted the location of the truck, got out of

the program, turned off the computer, pulled the shop door securely behind her, and went home.

Sera was sitting on the couch with a throw over her and her cell in her hand when Edie opened the front door. "Any luck?"

"He wasn't at the shop. Wouldn't you be more comfortable sleeping in my bed?" asked Edie on the way to her bedroom.

Sera followed her. "I don't think I can sleep. What are you going to do?"

"Find Phil. His last known location was in the Deansville Marsh," said Edie, as she checked the working condition of the flashlight she kept at her bedside. It worked. She threw it on the bed.

"What's he doing there?"

"Don't know. I'm going to find that out."

Edie took the gun safe from the back of the highest shelf in her closet, unlocked it, removed her 9mm pistol and two magazines filled with bullets, and placed them next to the flashlight.

"Are you expecting trouble?" asked Sera.

"No, and I'm hoping it won't find me. Best to be prepared, though."

She pulled off the sweatshirt and the shirt. Rummaged through her dresser, found a light wool sweater and put it on.

"Wool? In this heat?"

"I'm going into a marsh and don't know what I'll find there. In this scenario, wool is better than cotton." Edie picked up the flashlight, gun, and magazines off her bed.

"Is Phil okay?"

"Don't know, that's why I'm going," said Edie, peeping into Hillary's bedroom. Her daughter was still sleeping.

Sera followed her to the front door.

Edie took a running jacket from the closet, put the gun and magazines in the back pocket, the flashlight in a side pocket, and put her cell in her back jean pocket.

"Are you really going to need all that?"

"I hope not, but it's been one crazy week that I've been having."

Chapter 33

†

Edie turned on the GPS system in her car, the one that Phil had installed and she had never used. She keyed in the number of the Rooster's Crow Bar, and she saw that it anchored the southeast end of the Berlin Road. She consulted her paper map and laid it on the seat next to her. Edie always had a paper map with her. She never trusted a GPS system, too many stories of people driving off cliffs, ditches, or into oceans—it was a case of verifying before trusting and following its instructions. Then Edie backed out of her driveway.

Tonight Edie was glad for the company of the GPS and its authoritative female voice as she drove through the quiet dark backroads of Dane County. The sparse farm lights guided her through the twists and turns of Greenway Road. When the GPS instructed her to turn right, Edie ignored it. She hadn't seen a road where the GPS told her to turn, only darkness. She drove a mile down the road. Edie pulled over and consulted a map. Damn, that GPS was correct. She had taken one turn too many, she should have taken that right turn into oblivion.

At the next farm field entrance, Edie turned around and followed the GPS directions. She did what she was told and drove off the edge of the world into the Deansville Wildlife Area. Though farm lights dotted the rim of the almost two thousand acres of the designated wildlife area, they couldn't pierce the darkness of the hole. Her car lights were her only guide.

The first bullet took out her right headlight. The second bullet, the left. Edie's next movements were seamless. She maneuvered the car off the gravel road onto the shoulder and felt the right front drop, then heard a splash. "What is it? A puddle, pond, lake, river, or ditch?" she whispered to herself. "It doesn't matter; this car isn't any good to me now." She dropped to the car seat, opened the passenger-side door, and tried to calculate how far the drop would be. "Well, Edie, it doesn't matter, you stay here and you are dead." She slid into the water. "My mistake, this isn't water, it's slime." She stayed low and tried to keep her face out of the slime and her movements controlled. She didn't want whoever was out there to hear anything, especially not a splash. A few more seconds and she touched the other side. She pulled herself up and crawled a few feet into the tall grasses. She pulled the grasses down, crawling on top of them to stay out of the muck. Yet the muck still seeped through. Edie stayed put, she couldn't see a thing in the dark. As she waited for her night vision to kick in, she listened to the night music provided by crickets, owls, and a few coyotes singing. They were comforting sounds, but she wished they would shut up; she needed to hear the sounds of whoever shot out her headlights.

She heard them. Gravel hitting gravel, someone or something was on the road. Edie backed deeper into the grasslands, at about sixteen feet she turned right, and started for the line of trees that had become visible. Her arm slid into slime. A "Goddamn it," escaped her; she hoped it wasn't echoing through the marsh. A hand grabbed her arm. She yanked back her arm, and then flipped onto her back, pivoted around, and kicked. And kicked. And kicked until her foot hit something soft, and then sank to the bone beneath it.

"You motherfucking Goddamn goon."

"Phil?"

"Edie?"

"Yeah, now shut up. I'm sure everyone in India heard you."

Phil dropped his voice. "Give me a hand up; I want to get out of this piss hole."

Edie dragged him out of the ditch and into the grasses.

"I think you broke my nose."

Edie flopped down next to him. "What have you been saying about my choice of words?"

"Why? Hillary isn't here, is she?"

"I'm not a fool; she's at home with Sera. Anything wet and sticky dripping from your nose?" she whispered in his ear.

"Not yet, but it hurts like hell."

"If you don't start whispering, in a moment it won't matter."

"What do you mean?"

"Someone's out there, they shot out my headlights. Looks like my being here was planned."

Edie and Phil were quiet for a moment as the implications of that sank in. August night sounds echoed across the marsh.

"What are you doing out here?" asked Edie.

"Trying to get home."

"From where?"

"Rooster's."

Edie wanted to punch him in the arm, but didn't—he'd only howl like a baby. "How many beers did you have?"

"A few."

"Two or three or a Wisconsin few?"

It was a moment before Phil fessed up. "A Wisconsin few."

"How'd you get into the ditch?"

"I fell into it. I think a tire blew, flew into a patch of cattails back a ways. Woke up out of the truck, staring at the stars. Fuck, that truck is probably totaled. Shit, my insurance will skyrocket."

"Focus on the positive; you're lucky you're alive. What's the rest of the story?"

"Don't really know. When I came to I was on the ground. Tried to stand, couldn't—think something's wrong with my ankle. So I crawled."

Edie said nothing.

Phil filled in the silent spaces. "Anyway, thought I'd try to make it to one of those houses on the rim, it was really slow going. It wasn't till I fell into the ditch that I made much progress. I'm happy to be out of that slime. Funny, I used to think getting slimed was hilarious."

"Where's your phone?" Edie wanted to keep their conversation to the essentials.

"Not in my pocket, maybe back at Rooster's Crow or in the truck, maybe somewhere in the cattails. What are you doing here?"

"Looking for you." Edie pulled her gun out of the back pocket and slammed a magazine into it.

"With a gun?"

"With the week I've been having, yeah. Hold this while I check out your nose and ankle." Edie handed the gun to Phil. "You know how to use this, right?" Words weren't needed, Edie felt the swear words silently directed at her by Phil.

When the tension between them eased, Phil turned toward Edie. She did a quick assessment of the injured sites.

"Nose not out of joint, can't say the same about your ankle. And you stink."

"Crawling through a marsh does that to you."

"Shhh."

This time they heard the death screams of a rabbit.

"Phil, we need to get out of here. Think you can move?"

"I've come this far—"

Edie slid her hand over his mouth. They heard the sound of gravel hitting gravel. It stopped. A few moments later, it started again.

"What's going on?" Phil whispered.

"Gravel's being kicked up."

"By what?"

"Most likely human, but I can't be certain, too far away. Keep quiet. Can you push yourself farther into the brush?"

Phil groaned every time he moved.

In a second, Edie was beside him. She put her hand over his mouth and whispered in his ear. "Stop. You're making too much noise."

"Can't help it, my leg hurts every time I move."

"Whoever is on the road is closer. Shhh."

Both were still as they listened for footsteps.

"Idiot, pick up your feet," said a male voice from somewhere on the road.

"Don't tell me what to do, you ain't my mother," the other man said, loudly.

"Shut up, or I'll shut you up. One more dead guy ain't going to make a difference tonight. Not a bad idea, then the money would be all mine."

After that, there was silence.

Edie tried to distinguish between the voices, something to identify them if they ever got out of the marsh. No...when they got out of the marsh.

"Shut up yourself. There's only one person in this mosquito hellhole to hear us, and soon she won't be talking."

"Ain't it enough that he's dead?"

"As long as I get the money, I don't ask questions. You shouldn't either."

"Why a cop?"

"Paid to do the work, not figure stuff out—same as you. But nearest I come to it, seems like maybe she's pissed someone off. Looking too deep into something, poking her nose where it shouldn't be—you know what I mean? What cop hasn't pissed someone off? No more questions, knowing too much ain't good for your health."

"Who's going to tell?"

"No more questions. We gotta find her."

Edie gave up, assigned them voice one and voice two.

"Two people," whispered Phil.

Edie kept the "duh" to herself.

"Don't be so sure, I've heard she's a wily one," said voice two.

Edie felt Phil jabbing her in the ribs. She kept quiet.

"Don't care. There's only one way in and one way out, and we've got both of them covered," said voice one.

"She could have gone cross-country in this marshy bit," said voice two.

"A girl walking through this muck? Don't count on it."

"I've heard different. Heard that she's a wild-cat. Maybe we should go back to where that delivery truck is. She came this far looking for him, maybe she made it back there," replied voice one.

"Worth a try, she sure ain't here."

For a moment, only the nocturnal symphony filled the night. Then they heard the sound of gravel hitting gravel—it was moving away from them.

"Let's recap what just happened," said Phil.

"My new truck was probably totaled because I was the bait to lure you here."

"If you read between the lines...yeah," said Edie.

"Why you?"

"No idea. But they've given us some time to plan our next move. You okay here?"

"Where you going?"

"See if I can figure a way out of here," said Edie, starting to pull herself toward the gravel road.

"Stay a moment," said Phil.

"Can't."

"Edie, they'll be back when they find that neither of us are near my truck."

"You're right, we don't have all night. I've got to get us out of here. I don't want our baby to be an orphan."

"Wait."

"What do you have to tell me, Phil? Please don't tell me that your life just flashed before your eyes. I don't want confirmation that I'm going to die here."

"I've got a few things to say in case that un-thinkable thing happens," said Phil.

"I'd like to get out of this. I may have been lured here, but I don't have to play by their rules. Can't it wait?"

"No."

Edie crawled back to him. "Well, might as well

255

die together. But they're going to know they've been in a fight. Who did we appoint as Hillary's guardian?"

"Don't remember; hope it was a good person. I'll review it when we get home. I pity those poor bastards."

"Damn, what day is it?"

"Saturday, maybe Sunday, I've lost track of time. Why?"

"If it's Sunday, my date with Aunt Jill isn't going to happen. Now, what do you have to tell me?"

The crickets chirped and the fireflies blinked while Edie waited for Phil to speak.

"I was drowning until I met you."

Edie moved closer to him. "I know, I pulled you out of the ditch and I can still smell you."

"Edie, you know what I mean. The past was drowning me when I met you. Edie, you blew away the cobwebs." Phil stopped for a few seconds. "That's a mixed metaphor, may my high school English teachers forgive me. I'd never met anyone like you. You were the future. I guess I've been trying to catch lightning in a bottle just for me."

"You must have a concussion; I barely followed you through all those twists and turns. If I'm the future, then how come you can't get past all that *kinder, kuche*, and *kirche* stuff?"

"It was what I was brought up on."

"Well, I wasn't."

"But yet you stayed with me. Why?"

"I've heard about this true confession game—never wanted to play it."

"Not even with me?"

"Some things are better left in the past."

"Edie, this is important. Why'd you stay with me?"

"At the possible end of our lives, you want a philosophical discussion?"

"Yes, I want to know why you stayed."

"Who can really pinpoint their attraction to another person? But I've been trying to figure that out. Why you? You were sleeping off a drunk when I arrested you. One strike against you. You got a clingy, opinionated mother. Another strike against you."

"Anything positive about me?" asked Phil.

"Maybe I stay with you because you are cute, sweet, and funny, or maybe you intrigue me." Edie stared at him for a long moment. "Phil, I've been thinking," she stopped in midsentence.

"What are you thinking?"

"Shhh." Edie focused on the trees across the road. A figure moved out of their shadow. She heard a gun fire and felt dirt burst into her face. "Police," she shouted as she raised herself to her knees. She sank further into the muck, but remained steady. Bullets were landing around her. Christ, what lousy shots. Here I am as exposed and as big as the broadside of the barn and they can't hit me, she said to herself. Edie returned fire until she heard a scream and a thud as a body hit the ground.

Police sirens drowned out the crickets. Red and blue lights flashed from the west where the road dropped into oblivion. Headlights from the east flooded the area.

Edie gave her gun to Phil, tried to stand up, gave up, and crawled through the grass until she came to the ditch. She sat on its edge and held her hands high. "Over here," she yelled.

"Well, what do we have here?" answered Gracie.

Chapter 34

†

Gracie walked until she stood directly across from Edie, the ditch between them. "Out for a midnight stroll, Edie?"

"Think you'll find a body somewhere on your side of this slime."

"Got that one."

"There's another man on the road somewhere east of here. I think he's armed."

Gracie sent deputies back to search for him. "This is another fine mess you got me into, Detective Swift. Another boatload of paperwork awaits us. Edie, you know the drill, I need you to hand over your gun."

"Can't give you what I don't have. But I can get it for you." Edie disappeared back into the grasses. She returned, half pulling Phil through the muck.

"Who do you have with you?" Gracie yelled.

"Phil. We'll be over in a minute. Sorry about this, Phil, but we've got to go through this ditch to get to the road on the other side." Edie helped Phil lower into the water, sliding in beside him. Phil relaxed, rested his head on her shoulder, and let Edie pull him over to the far side.

Gracie knelt down, grabbed Phil under the shoulders, and held him while Edie kicked herself out of the ditch. Together, she and Gracie lifted Phil out of the slimy water and onto the gravel road.

"What are you doing here, Gracie?" asked Edie, retrieving the gun from Phil and handing it over to Gracie.

"Thought I was rescuing you, again," said Gracie, watching Edie do a quick assessment of Phil's lower leg.

"How'd you know I was here?"

"Your neighbor, Seraphina Voss, called me. Said she was having a déjà vu moment about the two of you. Seraphina, that's a nice name... should've named one of my daughters that."

"Don't tell Sera that, she hates the name," said Edie.

"We either live with whatever our parents name us or not. How's Phil's leg?"

"Broken."

"I'll call for an ambulance," said Gracie.

"Make that two, Lieutenant," said Johnson, coming up beside her.

"He still living?" asked Gracie.

"Yes. We're doing some first aid now. Edie, how are you doing? Is that Phil with you?" asked Johnson.

"I'll be fine, and, yes, Phil is with me," replied Edie, pushing herself into a half kneeling position.

Phil put a hand on Edie's knee as she pushed herself off the ground. "Stay a moment longer, Edie. I got a feeling back there that you were going to ask me something before we were interrupted."

"It can wait," said Edie.

"I can't," said Phil.

"You two need some privacy?" asked Gracie.

"I don't. How about you, Edie?" asked Phil.

"No. On second thought, I need witnesses because I am about to take back all of those nice things I said about you."

"I doubt you're going to do that, but I think I need the witnesses, too," said Phil.

Gracie took a step back to take a look at Edie and Phil; they seemed to be locked in a world made for two. She smiled. "Edie, looks like you need my help. Phil, will you marry Edie?"

"Gracie, it doesn't count if you ask me," said Phil.

"Since Edie will be going on administrative leave, thought I'd shorten the engagement time—give you more time for your honeymoon. And I'm warning you, Phil; damn you isn't a good way to start any relationship, especially marriage. Give it some good hard thinking before you say anything," said Gracie.

Edie stood up.

"She hasn't said it yet, but if she does, I'll take it. Even with a damn," said Phil.

"She will say it, I'll bet on it, probably be the first words out of that gutter mouth she's worked overtime this week," said Gracie.

"You've noticed that, too?" asked Phil.

Edie walked away from Phil and Gracie; she was a few hundred feet away before they noticed her missing.

"Where are you going?" Phil noticed she was gone and called after her.

"See if the other officers need some help with first aid," Edie called back.

"But we were talking," said Phil.

"No, *we* weren't, you and Gracie were."

"About our future."

"Yours and Gracie's? I'm not sure how Martin will take being supplanted, unless Gracie is going to become a bigamist."

"Ours. We were talking about you and me."

"Excuse me, when did that conversation involve you, me, and Gracie?" Edie asked, walking back to Phil and Gracie.

"When I had to rescue the two of you," said Gracie. "I hear some sirens. That'll be the ambulances. Edie, you need to wrap up this conversation fast."

"Phil, that future you were planning with Gracie about our future, without my consent, is fast disappearing," said Edie.

"Why?"

"Let me count the ways, Phil. You live in the past. You thought it was okay to talk about our future as if I wasn't around," said Edie.

"Don't forget he rescued you once upon a time. Give him a break," said Gracie, putting herself back into the conversation.

"And I just rescued him," Edie said, turning to Gracie. "And boss, it's time you butted out of this conversation."

"What about me? Where do you and I stand?" Phil asked.

"Right now, you've got no leg to stand on," Edie pointed out. She took a deep breath and started again. "Damn you, Phil."

Gracie interrupted her. "I knew it. Edie, I'm tired of all the gutter language that's been thrown around recently. Those words are not a good way of starting a marriage. Start over, Edie."

"How do you know what I was going to say?" demanded Edie.

"It's been obvious to everyone but you," said Gracie.

"Who's doing the asking, me or you, Gracie?"

"Edie, I'm just saying...."

Edie started over. "Phil, the future is always up for grabs. Not much certainty in it. But I'm crazy enough to do this. Phil, will you marry me?"

"Thought you'd never ask."

The End

About the author

Julia Hoffman lives with her family in the farm country of Wisconsin. And writes when not interrupted by a multitude of things.

Made in the
USA
Middletown, DE